"I have altered my previous opinion."

Rafael stared down at the silent Mary in the creamy moonlight.

"Taking everything into consideration," he went on, "I have come to the conclusion that I must take a wife. I am asking you if you will do me the honor of accepting my proposal."

At that moment Mary was incapable of accepting anything, let alone a proposal of marriage from the daunting Rafael Alvarados.

"I don't...I really...." She made a tremendous effort to pull herself together and tried again. "You must see that I'm completely overwhelmed. I'm very grateful, of course—and honored," she added hastily as an afterthought, "but marriage...!"

Her intensity surprised Rafael. It was a new experience for him to find someone as wary of the marital state as he had once been.

OTHER
Harlequin Romances
by JANE CORRIE

The Spanish Uncle

by

JANE CORRIE

Harlequin Books

TORONTO•LONDON•NEW YORK•AMSTERDAM
SYDNEY•HAMBURG•PARIS•STOCKHOLM

Original hardcover edition published in 1979
by Mills & Boon Limited

ISBN 0-373-02313-8

Harlequin edition published February 1980

Printed in U.S.A.

CHAPTER ONE

MARY ALLIS gave an exasperated sigh. Where had Paul got to? Her eyes scanned the visitors to the exhibition, milling in and out of the entrance hall. He had been there a moment or so ago—she really must curb this tendency of his to wander off when something caught his eye. Then she saw him; he had evidently gone back for another look at the wine pressing section—she remembered that he had been fascinated by it.

Her fine grey eyes took in the slight figure that had not as yet seen her as he stood forlornly looking about him. 'I'm over here, Paul,' she called. She smiled at the way his eyes lit up as he saw her and rushed towards her. 'Darling, I do wish you wouldn't wander,' she scolded him. 'We've only just time to make the bus— come on!'

With his hand firmly tucked into hers, Mary turned towards the exit and cannoned into a tall man entering the exhibition. 'I'm terribly sorry——' she began as her glance met his face, then she stopped dead and just stared, for she was looking at an exact replica of what Paul would look like in twenty years' time. As her startled eyes took in the amazing resemblance, a note of fear struck her heart and she clutched Paul's hand tightly and made for the door.

'One moment, please,' she heard a deep voice intone, but she did not turn round, for she was sure that she knew who had spoken. The deep voice had held a slight accent, but fear kept her going and she pretended that she had not heard the request.

'Mummy, that man wants to speak to you,' said Paul, looking back at the man, but Mary muttered something about missing the bus if they did not hurry, and carried on, only to find her way blocked once more by that exceedingly tall man.

'I—we have a bus to catch,' she said breathlessly. 'I'm sorry, but it's imperative that we catch it,' and she made to dart past the man, but he stood his ground.

'I'll see you get to your destination,' he said calmly yet firmly. 'I do think we ought to have a talk, don't you?' His eyes were on Paul as he spoke, and without waiting for Mary's agreement caught her arm lightly but firmly and turned her towards the hall again. 'If you would be so good,' he said authoritatively, and led her towards an office section beyond the main exhibition hall.

Without making a scene, there was not a lot Mary could do about it. If only Paul had not wandered off, she thought miserably, but it was all 'ifs'. If she hadn't taken him to see that exhibition. If there had been any other exhibition on at that particular time; there were any amount of 'ifs', but it didn't help her to recall any of them at that particular time. All she knew was that she had to have her wits about her. Whatever the man said, he had no rights where Paul was concerned; not after all this time. He was hers, and she would fight for him. Not even if he was the father—it made no difference—not now.

Paul, whose eyes had never left the man's face, voiced her sentiments in the most embarrassing way, but typically childlike. 'Are you my father?' he asked suddenly, as the man guided them towards a door at the end of the long corridor.

Mary closed her eyes. 'Hush, Paul!' she said quickly, thanking providence that there were no visitors within proximity.

The man smiled down at Paul, and Mary noticed how his austere face softened as he looked at the child. 'No,' he replied quietly, 'but I do know who your father was.'

Mary's heart lifted temporarily; he wasn't the father, and that meant that he couldn't make life difficult for her. Did that mean that Enrique was dead? She glanced swiftly at the man now opening the door for them; he was so like Paul that he must be Enrique's brother, the likeness was so striking it could be no other. Her lips straightened; that meant that he was Paul's uncle, and as she was his aunt, he had no legal rights over her.

Even as they entered the room the man still kept a light hold on Mary's arm as if afraid she might suddenly make a bolt for it, although how, as he had now closed the door behind them, Mary was at a loss to understand, but she was well aware of his determination in keeping his quarry in close proximity.

The room was a small office, and after a courteous request that she should be seated, the man seated himself behind the desk and addressed Paul, who appeared unable to take his eyes off the man he so closely resembled. 'So your name is Paul, is it?' the man asked, giving the boy a brief smile.

Paul nodded, then stuck his chin out in what Mary recognised as a haughty gesture of his when faced with something he did not understand and not liking the disadvantage, as young as he was. 'I like my first name bestest,' he answered solemnly. 'It's Enrique,' and fixing his large dark eyes on the man he asked, 'What's yours?'

Again that brief smile lit the man's hard face, and it occurred to Mary that this man did not indulge often in the practice of salutary greetings. 'My name is Rafael. You may call me Uncle Rafael. Your father was my brother, so that is quite in order.'

Mary intervened quickly here, afraid that Paul might ask further embarrassing questions. 'That's enough, Paul. Be a good boy and just keep quiet while Mr——' she stopped short in total embarrassment, she did not know the man's surname, and a painful flush washed over her cheeks.

The man's cold black eyes met hers briefly before he gave what Mary could only describe as a slight bow, and supplied with what sounded suspiciously like a kind of disdain that heightened the colour in Mary's cheeks, 'Rafael Esteban Alvarados, at your service, *señora*,' and held out a strong lean hand towards her.

Mary placed her small hand in his and returned the compliment, if it was a compliment, for she realised that he had addressed her as a married woman, and acting purely on instinct she did not correct this error, but keeping her left hand close to her side and away from surveyance, she murmured, 'Er—Allis, Mary,' and took it from there, surreptitiously turning her engagement ring round so that only the metal band was presented.

After the introductions had been performed, Mary sat back and made a point of glancing at her watch. Whatever the man had to say to her she wished he would get it over with. Perhaps he would suggest that he keep in touch with them, and she had no quarrel with this sentiment as long as that was all he wanted, but she could not convince herself of this. The man's very presence threatened her peace of mind, though why she should be so afraid she had no idea. It was a little late in the day for the family of Enrique to take an interest in his son when they had turned their backs on the girl whose child he had fathered. Her lips thinned as she thought of Sheila, who had been so trusting and so gullible, and who had never once in her short period of motherhood accepted the fact that her Enrique had feet of clay and had walked out on her, ostensibly to return to Spain to gain his father's permission to marry, as he had put it to the trusting Sheila, the woman he loved, and to seek his release from the girl chosen by his family to become his wife.

Her somewhat bitter musings were interrupted by the man sitting opposite her as he leaned forward and pressed a bell on the desk in front of him. 'Do you like ice cream, Enrique?' he asked the still puzzled boy, whose face lit up in expectation at the query, and who nodded fervently in answer.

Mary, taking full note of the way the man addressed Paul by his first name, felt a spurt of annoyance at the autocratic way he had bypassed the name 'Paul' as if it were of no consequence and put his implacable stamp on future proceedings. She said quickly, 'It's a little near our evening meal, dear,' and gave the man a challenging look as if daring him to override her in this.

He not only dared, but completely ignored the silent challenge Mary had thrown out by addressing the person who had answered the bell and issuing instructions to him that he was to accompany Master Enrique to the refreshment table and provide him with an ice. In answer to Mary's tight-lipped glare at this flagrant disregard to her wishes, he said lightly, 'I'm sure one ice would not spoil the young man's appetite,' then addressed the man whose eyes lingered on Paul for a moment and then returned to Rafael Alvarados. 'Take your time, Miguel, will you?' He glanced at the fine gold watch on his wrist. 'Fifteen minutes at least, please,' he ordered.

The man nodded his understanding, and inclined his head at Paul. 'Shall we go?' he said, his heavy sober countenance breaking into a smile purely in an effort to gain the child's confidence.

To give Paul credit, he did hesitate and look at Mary, seeking her permission to sample the treat in store, and again she felt that unreasonable spurt of fear. But was it so unreasonable? What was to stop the man from walking away with Paul and out of her life? She swallowed and looked back at Rafael Alvarados, and there must have been something in the look that she gave him that made him say abruptly, 'I give my word he shall be brought back here directly,' his dark hard eyes boring into hers as if willing her to trust him.

With a faint shock Mary realised that she did trust him; she did not like him, there was something altogether too overpowering about him that slightly frightened her, but she nodded at Paul and watched them leave, Paul with his small hand trustingly placed in the large hand of the thick-set man addressed as Miguel.

There was a tiny silence in the office after their departure, and Mary, marshalling her wits ready for what she now sensed to be some kind of battle over Paul's future, cast a quick assessing look at Rafael Alvarados, and noted with no little confusion that he was subjecting her to a minute scrutiny.

Although his face was completely bland, and she could discern no emotion whatsoever that gave her the slightest hint as to his thoughts, she sensed a certain amount of puzzlement in his assessment of her, and she wondered why.

He looked away abruptly from her wary eyes and studied the desk top, as if seeking the right approach to what, after all was said and done, could be a highly embarrassing conversation, at least it appeared so from his way of thinking, and Mary was fully aware of this. 'The child would be seven years old now, wouldn't he?' he said abruptly, cutting into Mary's reflection of his dark forbidding features.

Mary's sardonic eyes met his. 'I'm surprised you know that much,' she said, forcing a note of dryness into her voice and willing herself to remain calm and dignified over the matter. It was no use dragging the bitterness back, but for Sheila's sake she would lose no opportunity in showing this proud and obviously wealthy family that they had no need of their patronage, as hard as it had been for Mary to bring Paul up.

Rafael Alvarados's eyebrows quirked up at the corners at this blunt remark of hers, and his hard firm lips straightened for a second or so, proving to Mary how distasteful he found the whole business, but she had not sought this interview, he had brought this on his own head. 'It may interest you to know that an exhaustive search was made for you and the child when Enrique's effects were forwarded to my father.'

He was silent for a moment or so, and then looked up suddenly at Mary, who couldn't see that that information meant anything relevant, as Enrique had still deserted Sheila. 'He died shortly after a motor accident on the way to see his father. Later, of course, we learnt the purpose of the visit. He wasn't due home until his studies ended in July.' He stared down at the desk again. 'We hadn't much to go on, you know. One letter, presumably from you,' he gave Mary a quick glance, 'but apart from the usual endearments, no name, and no address. We wouldn't have known about the child if Enrique hadn't left a message to be forwarded to my father.' He looked away again and firmed that strong jaw of his. 'There wasn't much time, you understand, and he knew this. By the time my father received the message it was probably out of its original context, but one thing was clear, he was desperately anxious that you and the child be provided for.'

Mary sat stunned, her wide eyes echoing her thoughts that alternated from shock to downright shame at the way she had misjudged Enrique. Sheila had known he wouldn't let her down, and how right she had been. Her eyes filled with tears as she thought of her sister, and how proud and happy she would have been at this moment if she had lived to hear this, but she had survived only a few months after having Paul, and Mary had brought him up, finding herself unable to give him up no matter how many problems it inevitably brought her.

In the midst of these heart-searching thoughts, one fact was clamouring for attention and eventually broke through her consciousness, and that was that Rafael Alvarados had assumed that she was Paul's mother. The tears slipped over and she dashed them away quickly, but her thoughts were still with her, and she couldn't so easily wipe them away. Wasn't she his mother? She hadn't given birth to him, but she had been there to hold out her arms to the small stumbling child as he had taken his first tentative steps under his own power. It was she who had seen him through all the childish ailments, she who had worried about his slow recuperation after whooping cough when he had been five. She swallowed the lump that had risen in her throat; there had been countless occasions that had bound him irretrievably to her, and she to him. She was mother to him, and always would be, so why should she deny the fact? It couldn't hurt anyone, not now. Sheila and Enrique had gone, but she and Paul still had each other —and there was Derek. She swallowed again. Odd that she should not give him a thought until now. When she married Derek, he would look after them. In the meantime she had to find something to say to the unexpected and entirely shaking news that she had just received. She looked up at the man who had sat so silently while she had marshalled her thoughts and found him studying a heavy gold ring on his little finger, yet she sensed his thoughts were far away. He could not have missed her emotional reaction to the news that he had given her, but she had no doubt that he had put another interpretation on it. If she had been Sheila, her thoughts would have been on Enrique and the fact that he had died all that time ago, and she had not known.

'I'm sorry,' she said in a low voice. 'I—well, the news came as a shock to me. I—we thought——' She hesitated here, realising she must be careful in what she said.

He nodded abruptly as if to assure her that it was not necessary for her to go on. 'As I have said,' he went on in that deep voice of his, 'all efforts to trace you petered out. It appeared that Enrique kept his affairs to himself. We could find no associate of his who knew either your name or your address.' He shrugged his wide powerful shoulders. 'Oh, they knew there was someone, but whoever she was, she was not a student at the university, that much was ascertained, so there was no help there.'

Mary looked away quickly; Sheila had met Enrique at an evening institute that she and Mary were attending in order to learn Spanish, and Enrique English. They had collided into each other at the entrance one evening, much as Mary had collided with Rafael and brought about this astonishing sequel to the past. In the case of Enrique and Sheila it had been love at first sight, not that Mary had believed in such a happening at the time. At nineteen, Sheila was two years younger than Mary, and Mary had thought that she was just indulging in a light flirtatious affair, for she was pretty enough to gain a lot of attention from the male sector of the population. It was not long afterwards that both were missing from their separate classes, having come to the joint decisi n that Enrique would teach Sheila Spanish, if she would teach him English, and as Mary had no wish to play gooseberry she had carried on at the institute to the successful conclusion of her course.

She roused herself from her reverie in time to make some reply to Enrique's brother who was still closely watching her. 'Oh, well, we moved away from the district anyway, and we—I,' she hastily corrected herself, 'didn't know anybody at the university.' She stared at the wall behind Rafael Alvarados before she continued; she was normally a very truthful person and was useless at any kind of subterfuge, but the thought of Paul and what she was fighting for gave her the courage to go through with it. 'When we—I heard nothing further from Enrique, we—I assumed that he had——' She swallowed, not knowing how to put their feelings at that time—well, at least, hers. Sheila had never doubted Enrique.

Another brief nod from Rafael Alvarados saved her the necessity of continuing and she was extremely grateful for this at least. She hoped he showed the same understanding with anything else connected with the past, for she doubted her ability to keep up the subterfuge that she had embarked upon.

'You did know he was engaged, didn't you?' he said quietly, bringing Mary back to the present with a jolt.

Mary nodded warily, and wondered why he should bring up that particular point now.

'I very much doubt whether he would have married you,' he continued slowly, his eyes dwelling on her face, no doubt to watch the reaction this calm statement brought, but Mary's face showed no emotion in spite of the fury she felt building up inside her. Sheila would not have been good enough for them, of course, and her soft lips firmed at the thought as she stared back coolly at the elegant man in front of her.

There must have been something in the calm way she had looked at him that prompted him to add, 'Perhaps I am wrong in this; but I do know my father would have opposed the marriage vigorously. On a point of honour, you understand?'

Again Mary nodded, and wished wearily that he would get to the point. Was he afraid that some claim would be made upon the family, and felt it necessary to point out a few salient facts? She would soon put him right on that, she thought bitterly; just let him offer her some recompense!

His light sensitive fingers made a quick impatient drumming sound on the desk that told her they had got to the crux of the meeting, and he was impatient to put his proposition, if that was what it was, before her. 'However, that is over and done with,' he commented firmly, 'and we have now found the child.' He looked up at Mary suddenly, and she had the impression that his next words were going to leave her in no doubt of his objective in seeking this interview with her.

'My father is now an old man, and his health is failing,' he said as he drew in a deep breath, 'and there is no doubt at all that once he learns of the existence of this child, he would want to see him. As there is no possibility of his making any journey in his state of health, I am asking you to consider taking the child to see him.'

At Mary's quick gasp of surprise he held up his hand. 'All expenses paid, of course.' He leaned forward and continued in a low vibrant voice, 'I beg you to consider this request favourably. Enrique's death hit him hard, and it would be a kindness that would greatly indebt me to you if you comply with my wishes in this.' He looked away from Mary and studied the desk top, and she sensed that he was struggling under some inward emotion, but was unwilling to show her this, it was also obvious that he thought a lot of his father. 'I realise that you have every right to refuse this request,' he went on in a low voice, 'but I do ask you to remember that efforts were made to carry out Enrique's wishes, and it was through no fault of ours that we failed. To say that this state of affairs caused my father much pain and anguish would be no untruth. He and Enrique were particularly close to one another. They were much alike in many ways. I can say in all honesty that since the death of Enrique life has not held a great amount of pleasure for him.' He looked down at his slim hands and gently flexed them. 'There were just the two of us, and I, for various reasons that are unnecessary to go into, disappointed him, and it was in Enrique that his hopes were centred.' He gave a light shrug, as if to throw off these memories. 'I feel that it is necessary for you to know these things, and that it is extremely likely that adequate provision will be made for the child.'

He took a deep breath. 'However, these things can be gone into later. All I ask now is that you should discuss this with your husband.' He raised his brows slightly, and waited for Mary's confirmation on this before going on.

Mary was now in a dilemma. She had already told one untruth, and didn't see how she could conjure up a husband, not without seeking Derek's complicity in the plot, and knowing Derek, she baulked at the idea. 'Er—fiancé,' she said quickly.

She did not fail to notice that her answer had given him some satisfaction, although his voice gave none of his thoughts away. 'Quite so,' he said easily. 'It is now I believe what is termed as the summer vacation period, is it not? and though I do not know what arrangements you have made for your holiday, I very much hope that you will consider my offer to spend a few weeks at my home in Seville.'

Mary sat in stunned silence. Events were happening much too fast for her, she needed time to assimilate the facts; whatever she had expected, it hadn't been this. She knew a deep sense of foreboding, as if she had suddenly stepped on to a roundabout and someone had altered the timing mechanism and she was now whirling around at great speed and unable to stop. She felt breathless and somehow totally inadequate to cope. She wanted to make excuses as to why it would be impossible for them to accept his offer, and put it off until perhaps next year—or the year after that, yet she knew that she couldn't. Without his actually belabouring the fact, she knew that Enrique's father was very ill, and had sensed the urgency behind his request. Her teeth caught her soft lower lip; she still needed time. She glanced up at Rafael Alvarados and saw how tensely he was watching her. 'I'll have to think about it,' she said slowly, adding a trifle lamely, 'I'm sorry about your father's poor health.'

Rafael Alvarados continued to look at her, and she knew that he was waiting for a definite answer from her, and she wished she had the courage to say no, there and then, but knew that he would accept no such answer and she really could not expect him to. 'I'm sorry,' she repeated hastily, 'but you must see all this has come as quite a shock to me. You must think me very unfeeling.' Her large eyes pleaded with him to understand, even though she sensed that he was not interested in her or her feelings, only in getting the right answer from her; a hard man, she thought, and one used to getting his own way.

He glanced at his watch before answering her. 'I assure you I have no wish to rush you into a decision here and now,' he said coolly. 'Enrique should be returning shortly. May I visit you, say, tomorrow evening, to discuss the matter further?' he asked.

So much for his assurance that he did not want to rush her, Mary thought crossly, yet it was precisely what he was doing, but at least she would be given a breathing space to think things out, and she gave a swift nod of agreement.

There was a tap on the door at this point, and after Rafael Alvarados had given the authoritative permission for entry, Paul was ushered in by Miguel. As they entered the office Rafael Alvarados stood up, showing

Mary that the interview was over for the time being at least, and that he was now ready to escort them home.

Mary sat in the back of the expensive-looking car, leaving Paul the honour of sitting up front beside his newly-discovered uncle, and after giving him her address, she felt a short spurt of surprise that he was so well acquainted with the outskirts of the vast city as to be in no need of further direction other than the mentioned district. To her further surprise, he caught her eye in the driving mirror and said calmly, 'I too attended university in England.'

Mary gave a short polite, 'Oh, did you?' and sank back in her seat and made a pretence of looking out of the window at the streaming traffic around them. So that was something else she had learnt about Rafael Alvarados, he might be a hard man, but he was also extremely observant—she did not think her face had been all that expressive. Her job as a teacher had taught her the necessity of keeping her emotions out of her expression, and up until now she had managed very efficiently.

Although her mind was teeming with the sudden development that had taken place in her and Paul's life, she resolutely pushed all these thoughts aside until she could give them due consideration in a more peaceful atmosphere, and thought about the tall dark man who was Enrique's brother.

To some he would have appeared handsome, if one was drawn to the dark satanic type. She winced at the description she had just labelled him with and wondered why such a thought had entered her head. No one would have thought Enrique a satanic type, yet he had had the same dark features, and the same high cheekbones with the black winged brows that were so expressive. Yet this man was no Enrique; Enrique had been a warm, impulsive man, and as it had turned out, a very loyal one to the woman he had loved.

Mary was sure one could not say the same of the man in front of her. This man was cold, and she wondered if he ever really smiled. She thought of his expression as he had looked at Paul; there had been a kind of tenderness there, she remembered, but only where the child was concerned, and because he was Enrique's child. Odd that he should have taken so strongly after his father in looks, and not his mother, although Sheila had been a brunette, it was true, but her complexion had been naturally pale, while Paul's was dark, as if he had a built-in honeyed tan that lasted all the year round.

She broke off her reverie to tell Paul not to be so inquisitive, and to stop asking his uncle so many questions and let him concentrate on the driving, but his uncle said he had no objection to the questions, so Mary was forced to leave them to it and only hope that no embarrassing ones were asked. Even if they were, she told herself sardonically, the smooth sophisticated Rafael Alvarados would know how to handle them, so why should she worry? She lapsed back into her reverie. How old was Rafael? If Enrique had lived he would be about thirty, Mary mused, and she had gathered that Rafael was the elder of the two brothers and that meant he was probably in his middle thirties. Married? She didn't think so, and she couldn't have said why. Was it because of something he had said about disappointing his father? She had also got the distinct impression that Paul was the only grandchild, and the thought gave her a nasty jolt as she also remembered what

Rafael had said about some provision being made for Paul.

'We have many vineyards,' commented the deep voice of the man Mary was trying to categorise. 'I shall show you round them when you come to Seville. You would like that, wouldn't you?' he asked in an amused way.

Paul's ecstatically breathed, 'Oh, yes!' gave Mary another hard jolt and with it a sense of panic. They were as good as on the plane now, she was certain of it. She was also certain that nothing would ever be the same again. She would lose Paul, they would take him away from her. They could offer him so much more than she could. It was as well for her that they had arrived at their destination, for she knew a sudden longing to stop events right there and then, to tell this strong hard man to stop the car and to get out and take Paul with her and just walk off and lose themselves in the thronging mill of humanity and out of reach of Rafael Alvarados.

CHAPTER TWO

LATER that evening a mentally exhausted Mary settled herself down in their small sitting-room and gave her thoughts full rein without fear of disturbance.

Paul had been coerced to bed at his normal time, although he plainly thought that Mary ought to have allowed him an extra half an hour in which to ply his endless questions about his father, and had eventually fallen asleep muttering something about did she know that they grew oranges out there? and fell asleep before she could answer, much to her relief.

As if she hadn't enough to worry about, another problem had now loomed on the horizon. She had always taught Paul to be truthful and never to shirk the consequences, yet here she was faced with her own dilemma on this strict observance. She had never told Paul that she was not his mother, there had never been occasion to. He had accepted her, as she had accepted him, as hers, although she had realised that one day she would have to tell him.

She stirred restlessly in her chair; he was only seven and surely there was time enough for such enlightenment. She sighed deeply. Perhaps she ought to have instilled it into him a long time ago, so that he could grow up in the knowledge, but it was too late for that now. She had to be thankful that he was a happy and contented child who had never whined about the loss of a father, even though she suspected that he must have wondered sometimes. She could only recall one occasion when he had asked about his father, and Mary had simply said, 'He's gone, darling. There's only you and me,' not realising at the time that she had spoken the truth without knowing it, but he had accepted it and given her a hug, as if to say that that was all right by him.

Her eyes misted over at this recollection; yes, there had been time enough for the truth to be told, but what now? How long could she keep it from him now? She thought of Rafael Alvarados and his sick father, and her full lips firmed. If Paul had been older, she would have no need of subterfuge, but he was still only a child with no one else to look out for him and his happiness came first—it always had done, even where Derek was concerned.

She stared at the print of a Constable above the fire-place, but for once the picture of the countryside and gently rolling hills did not give her the peace it usually did. She had been engaged to Derek for two years now, but had always managed to avert naming the day when she would become Mrs Handley. At first it had simply been good sense to wait until they had saved enough to buy a home of their own, although Derek had wanted them to move in with his mother, but Mary knew that Derek's mother had no time for children, and saw no pleasure in having to constantly tell Paul to, 'wipe your feet, dear,' or, 'Mrs Handley's got a headache, so don't laugh so loud, love.'

Of course, Derek could have moved in with Mary and Paul, but Derek taught at the local college and it would have meant a longer journey to work for him. There was also the undeniable fact that he felt that the district Mary lived in was not quite what might be described as a desirable one, and his mother would have been horrified at the thought of her son living in what she would describe as a 'downgraded area'. The plain fact was that Mrs Handley was a snob, and unfortunately Derek shared many of her views.

Mary eased the leg that she had tucked under her into a more comfortable position. She had a habit of sitting with one leg curled under her, a habit that she would have to cure if and when she married Derek, as there was no doubt that Mrs Handley would be a constant visitor, if only to assure herself that Derek was getting his full quota of vitamins, and she was a stickler for correctness.

She sighed. The 'if and when' problem had been with her for a long time, particularly the 'if', and now was as good a time to face it as any other since Paul and Derek did not get on together, but had suffered each other's company purely out of deference to Mary. A lot of it was jealousy, Mary had to admit, but she always contended that Derek ought to have recognised it as such and done something about it and eased the situation. However, she suspected it was a little more than that where Derek was concerned, and she was a little afraid that he shared his mother's views on the 'children should be seen and not heard' theme, although if this was put to him she was certain that he would strenuously deny it, but it was a fact that he resented Paul.

Mary had often wondered how they had got to the engaged state, for neither of them could be said to be passionately in love with the other. She supposed they had just drifted into it. For her it had been a kind of security. She had liked Derek and felt safe with him, and had not felt the need of a passionate attachment, particularly after what had happened to Sheila, but she would have been surprised if this fact had been pointed out to her. As far as she was concerned, her conservative outlook abhorred any emotional display, and if that was what love did to you, she would rather settle for the solid but dependable type of man, if a little dull at times. At least you knew where you were with them.

Her smooth forehead crinkled at this thought. Did she know where she was with Derek? Surely the fact that she hadn't been absolutely certain of what the future held for them had been the prime factor in her steadfastly refusing, or putting off taking the irrevocable step—not for herself but for Paul's sake, since Derek had shown definite signs of what he called 'taking him in hand' when they were married. The sad fact was that Derek had not got a sense of humour, and Paul had an impish one. He was not a naughty boy, but did take delight in childish pranks much as any child of his age would, but they were always met with a stony face from Derek and a muttered comment of how he wished the boy would grow up.

She shook her head impatiently. This was not getting her anywhere; she had other things to think of now such as what to do about Rafael Alvarados's invitation to spend part of their summer holidays in Seville. That they would go was certain, but for how long? Derek had planned to take Mary on a tour of Scotland and had insisted on her making arrangements to leave Paul with a friend of hers, Sarah Holland, for the week. This would not have been any hardship for Paul, since he would be staying with his best friend's family and would certainly enjoy the stay with them much more than finding himself constantly under the surveillance of an exasperated Derek, and not one of them would have enjoyed the holiday.

Mary had agreed to this arrangement since, as Derek had pointed out, he rarely saw her alone, not even in the evenings when he called on them, as Paul would inevitably make some demand on her attention from the well-worn excuse of 'could I have a drink of water,' down to another oldie, that he couldn't sleep. Mary might have been a little more strict with him had she not known that under these pathetic little excuses to gain her attention lay a much deeper cause, a sense of insecurity that had only come into being since Derek had entered their lives.

She smoothed her wide skirt over her knees. There was no denying that Paul was afraid for the future; he did not like Derek, and to be strictly honest, Derek had done nothing to erase his dislike, and certainly nothing to bring them into a closer understanding of each other. When they were together, Mary found she had to constantly watch points and act as a buffer between them, but she had never ceased to hope that one day something would happen to break the deadlock between them. It was during the holiday periods that she had pinned this rather forlorn hope. However, the previous year's fiasco had not given her much expectation of this, and had resulted in Derek insisting that Paul give them some peace and harass someone else.

Mary's worried glance rested on the small desk calendar on the bureau in front of her. It was now early July, and Derek had arranged for them to go on holiday the first week of August. That meant that she would not be able to accept the invitation from Rafael Alvarados until the middle of August, for she would need a week or two to arrange things her end. Her frown deepened. There wouldn't be much time for a long visit, as the school term began in the first week of September and she would have to be back for that.

She got up to make herself a cup of coffee; so that was that, she thought. It was the third week in August or nothing, unless they paid a visit during the Christmas recess. She shook her head impatiently at the thought. Of course they couldn't go away for Christmas, it was unthinkable, and Derek would certainly have something to say about that. It would have to be the third week in August, or some time next year. As she waited for the coffee percolater to start simmering, she had a feeling that Rafael Alvarados might have other ideas on the subject, but there was nothing he could do about it. She had a living to earn, and there was no way that she would allow Paul to remain in Spain without her, if such a suggestion were forwarded.

As she drank her coffee she felt a sense of foreboding, and wished that Derek were there to assure her in his usual bluff way that she had nothing to worry about, but three nights a week he gave private coaching lessons to budding mathematics students, and she would not see him until Thursday. Normally he would slip down to see her during the day, and she would have lunch with him, but this week his mother had made a prior claim, presenting him with a list of odd jobs to be done about the house, and wanting them done before he went away on holiday. She had done the same last year, and Mary suspected that it was just a ploy to keep him by her side. It was extremely annoying yet somehow pathetic, and was something else Mary would have to learn to cope with in time.

The following day the same feeling of uncertainty

haunted her as she carried out the usual household chores, but she was relieved of Paul's high-spirited presence, not to mention his excited comments at the thought of going to Spain, by Michael, his bosom pal, presenting himself at the door and asking if Paul could go on a picnic with them. Mary inwardly blessed her friend Sarah for the kind thought, and willingly gave her permission.

Paul arrived back just after six and Mary was gratified to see that he was quite worn out. He could hardly stay awake long enough to eat his supper, and she knew she would have no worry about him playing up later that evening when Rafael Alvarados called on her, and for this she was grateful.

As she looked down at his tousled dark head lying on the pillow, she wondered if he had forgotten that his uncle was due to pay them a visit that evening, but even if he had remembered, his obvious enjoyment of his day out had taken its natural course and he was oblivious to everything but the need to sleep.

She picked up his shorts, now streaked with mud in places, as were his socks and shoes, clear evidence of unrestrained happy activity, and placing the clothes in the laundry basket, she carried his shoes down to the kitchen to make them presentable for wear the following morning.

When this was done she went to her room and changed out of the old jumper and tweed skirt that she wore for household chores into a cotton dress, her thoughts all the time on the coming visit. It was when she was just giving herself a last-minute look in the mirror that she suddenly recalled Rafael Alvarados's look of puzzlement as he had studied her during that interview, and it suddenly struck her that he was obviously wondering just what his brother Enrique had seen in her. As her eyes met her own reflection, Mary gave a little grimace. Sheila had been the beauty of the family, and Mary not even an 'also ran'. Her features were regular but plain, her face just a little on the long side, and her full lips just a little too wide. Her thick chestnut hair was nothing out of the ordinary, although naturally wavy. Her wide grey eyes were her best feature, although she would not have agreed with this deduction; to her way of thinking she was just plain Mary Allis with no claim on the Venus stakes, and that suited her nicely.

At least it had until now; she could not alter her looks, neither could she expect to carry out her plan of deception without coming up against numerous barriers. It was not going to be easy, and it was going to be harder still when faced by Paul's grandfather who was, according to Rafael Alvarados, a sick man.

The thought made Mary quake inside. She wouldn't be able to go through with it, not if he was a kind man. She wouldn't be able to keep up the deception then, but would tell him the truth. If he was a good man, he would understand the reason for her deception, and surely he would not hold it against her. He would know that it was Paul's happiness she was concerned with, and if he was happy, then so was she.

Having somewhat stifled her conscience on this front, she went downstairs and awaited her visitor.

The doorbell rang prompt at eight o'clock, and Mary wondered if he had been standing outside the house waiting until the hands of his watch had pointed to eight, and then rung the bell, he was so punctual, and with a fluttery feeling inside her stomach she went to answer the door and admit him.

As she showed him into her small sitting-room she was once again struck by his height, and his immaculate appearance. His dark blue town suit fitted his powerful body with such elegance that it must have been tailor-made. His sky blue shirt emphasised his hard tanned features and his blue-black hair, so like Paul's, was brushed back from his forehead, yet Mary knew exactly what it would look like if left to its own devices and would fall over his forehead. The thought made her feel intensely uncomfortable and she didn't know why. Paul was so like him, these comparisons were inevitable, yet she didn't like them and hastily thrust the thought out of her mind.

With studious politeness he indicated that she should enter the room first, and then followed her, and for a moment or two after they had seated themselves there was a kind of tenseness between them and Mary saw him glance briefly round the room, and wondered what he made of what, from his point of view, must be a very humble abode.

'You have talked the matter over with your fiancé?' he asked.

Mary gave a start. She hadn't, of course, but it did not matter, for the decision remained entirely hers and whatever she decided, Derek would go along with her. However, she did not say this, but just nodded, then said quickly, 'I'm afraid we can only visit your home in late August, and then only for a week.' On seeing the quick frown this brought from him, she hurried on, 'I'm a teacher, you see, and I'll have to be back for work during the first week of September. There's also,' she carried on before he could interrupt her, 'the fact that we'd planned a holiday at the beginning of August,

Derek is taking me on a tour and all the arrangements are made.'

As she said this she suddenly realised that she had not mentioned the arrangements for Paul, and if Rafael Alvarados knew that Paul was not going to accompany them, he might very well suggest taking him to Spain for that week, which was something Mary did not want to happen, so she hastily added Paul's name, 'That is, Paul and I,' wondering if her telltale flush had given her away and miserably wishing she could tell the truth. It was surprising the number of lies one had to tell, even on small things, and she had no taste for it.

She couldn't see what else she could add, although it was clear that Rafael Alvarados was displeased, and it occurred to her that he must think them very unfeeling where his father was concerned, so she felt obliged to add, 'We could come early next year, say, the Easter break, if that would be convenient?'

Rafael Alvarados did not answer immediately but looked down at his long slim fingers resting on the arm of his chair, and Mary had a feeling that he was not finding it easy to contain his thoughts on the matter that were plainly causing him some annoyance. 'I do understand it is difficult for you,' he said in his deep voice, 'but I hope you will see how difficult it will be for my father to understand that he will not be seeing the child for at least a month, and then only for a week.' He looked back at Mary. 'I did tell you that he was ill, did I not?' Mary nodded, wondering what was coming next. 'And I think I also explained that a lot of his ilness is due,' he shrugged his powerful shoulders, 'shall we say, to a kind of lethargy. In other words, he badly needs an interest in life.'

His brows lifted in an impatient manner. 'I can't put

it any other way, but I am certain,' his eyes bored into Mary's, 'that once he has seen the child who is so like Enrique, there is a great chance of him recovering his health. He is an old man, Miss Allis.' As before, this address was given as an unspoken question and Mary slightly inclined her head to show him that he had addressed her correctly. 'At least,' he went on, 'I hope he will fare as well as any man of his age. I am not saying he has fallen into a state of utter dejection and is malingering. He is a sick man, I can assure you of this, but in all of us there must be something to keep us going. Some reason, if you like, why we should want to get better. My father has not got that reason, or at least he hadn't, until now. Now that we have found Enrique's son, there is every chance of his enjoying the twilight of his life, but time is of the essence.'

He stopped suddenly and Mary realised that in a way he was pleading with her, and it was a role that did not come easy to him. She felt a stab of remorse as indeed he had meant her to, and she remembered what he had said about trying to find them all those years ago and couldn't see how she could refuse to fall in with whatever he had in mind.

She looked away quickly from his strong face and his dark eyes that seemed to bore right into hers, and clenched her hands together tightly. 'I see,' she said quietly, and moistened her lips before adding, 'Perhaps if you'll give me a week to make arrangements this end,' she hesitated, 'it might be possible to fit in a visit this month, but we shall have to be back by the first week of August for the holiday I mentioned to you earlier.'

'Thank you,' he said in a manner that showed his satisfaction with this reply. 'I am much obliged to you, and I can assure you of a very warm welcome from my father.' He stood up and felt in his jacket pocket and produced a wallet from which he took a card and handed it to her. 'If you run up against any snags, please let me know. Your passport is in order?' he asked abruptly.

Mary gave a quick 'yes'; she had taken Paul on a school outing to France the previous year. At this, he said crisply, 'Good! Well, if there is anything else you need, just contact me. I shall hold myself in readiness to escort you to my home. If you would contact me as soon as you are ready, I shall book the plane reservations and advise my father of the date of our arrival.'

That, it appeared, was that, and as Mary went to the door with him, she thought what an odd man he was. There must have been much he had wanted to know about them, yet he was obviously not going to seek the answers at that stage of their acquaintance. This suited her admirably as she would not have relished an inquisition on the past until she had got a few answers ready.

As she shook hands with him before his departure, she noticed that there was no sign of his car and presumed he had left it further up the street where the road was wider and would not cause an obstruction.

She had just returned to the sitting room when the front door bell pealed again, and thinking Rafael Alvarados had forgotten something, she went to answer it and found Derek on the doorstep. He gave her a puzzled look as he entered and asked curiously, 'Who was that man that just left? Looked a city type to me. Are you thinking of taking out more insurance?'

Mary gave a wry grin. 'It's a long story,' she said, following him into the sitting room. 'I didn't expect you this evening. Get through early, did you?' she asked.

He gave a grimace. 'There's a do on at the college, and no one thought to remind me that there'd be a skeleton attendance, so I packed the rest of them off to join in the festivities. They were longing to be off anyway.'

Mary told Derek of the surprising turn of events of the previous day, and he intervened every now and again with an astonished, 'Good lord!' and when she had finished he rubbed a hand through his brown hair in an abstracted fashion.

When she told him of her decision to take Paul to Spain some time the following week, she half expected him to protest or at least ponder on the advisability of rushing into things, but he said nothing, and in a way seemed pleased rather than displeased over the news.

'Well, that's normal, isn't it? I mean, they would want to see him, wouldn't they? I didn't get a good look at his uncle, only saw the back of him really, and he looks like Paul, you say?'

'Very much so,' replied Mary slowly, feeling slightly chagrined at Derek's calm way of taking her absence from the scene for what might turn out to be almost a month. 'Well, facially, at any rate,' she went on. 'There was no mistaking the fact that they were related, yet I think that's where the resemblance ends. From what I saw of his uncle, Rafael Alvarados, I formed the impression that he was not as easy-going as his brother was. In fact, he's quite a hard man, I would say.'

Derek shrugged as if her observations were of no consequence. 'They're not like us, are they? He is Spanish, after all,' he added, as if that explained everything.

Mary bristled at this cool summing up, and in some indefinable way knew that he had classed Paul in the

same category. However, there was no point in dwelling on that now. 'Anyway, we'll be back for our holiday
in August,' she told him. 'I made a point of insisting on
that.'

Derek gave her an assessing look. 'Suppose they
want to keep him there? If the old man's pining for the
son he's lost, I should think there's a good chance of
them offering to keep him. Let's see,' he went on
musingly, 'you'll be there almost a month, won't you?
Time enough for him to get to know the boy—and if
he takes a shine to him—Look here,' he added swiftly,
'if things are going well, don't worry about coming
back for our tour, we can always take it some other
time.'

'Some other time?' echoed Mary, although it wasn't
the holiday that filled her thoughts, it was his hope,
and that was exactly what it was, that they would take
Paul off her hands, but she swallowed the urge to shout
at him that she would allow no such thing and con-
centrated on the holiday. 'When? We're due back at
school in September, remember?'

'Oh, Easter, perhaps. There'll be plenty of time in
the future,' he answered laconically.

Mary's teeth clenched together. After Paul had gone,
was what he meant. 'If you're relying on the Alvarados
family taking Paul I can tell you here and now that I
have no intention of accepting such an offer, if they
make it; and I'm surprised at you for even thinking
that I might. Paul belongs to me, he always will do,' she
added fervently.

'Oh, come now,' replied Derek in what she recognised
as his soothing voice, 'let's use a little bit of sense here,
Mary. After all, I gather they're quite well off, aren't
they?'

Mary gave him a steady look. 'What's that got to do with it?' she demanded.

He gave a slight grimace. 'Quite a lot, I should have thought,' he said. 'It's his inheritance, isn't it—or at least it will be, if things go well. If you insist on keeping him tied to your apron strings he may very well lose it. Have you thought of that?' he demanded irritably.

Mary looked away quickly. 'Perhaps,' she answered slowly, 'but it depends on Paul, doesn't it? and whether he's happy or not—and he is happy, Derek.'

He made a noise that sounded like a snort of impatience. 'Well, of course he is, at the moment,' he snapped. 'You spoil him, Mary. I've always told you that, but later on—well, things won't quite be the same.'

Mary stared at him. 'What exactly do you mean by that?' she asked quietly.

'You know very well what I'm getting at,' he replied stiffly. 'I've never really had this out with you before. I've just let things go on, but I'm telling you now that if they do want to keep the boy I think it would be the best thing that could happen for all of us.'

'You mean let him go—just like that—because they're rich and I'm not, that's what it amounts to, doesn't it?' she cried, her voice slightly breaking even at the thought.

'I didn't mean that,' he answered hastily, 'not quite in that way. What I'm trying to say is, you must have seen that I don't get on with the boy. Oh, I've tried, but somehow we seem to be on different wavelengths. What I want you to think about is you and me, and our future.'

Mary looked away from him, not feeling able to face

him at that particular moment. He had, it seemed, a lot in common with Rafael Alvarados; both had resorted to a kind of moral blackmail to get what they wanted. 'I see,' she said in a low vibrant voice. 'You think that I should pack my things and Paul's, and off we go and hope that they take to Paul. Then I come back alone, to you. Is that what you have in mind?'

Derek's eyes met hers squarely. 'As a matter of fact, it is,' he replied challengingly.

Mary's composure left her. She wanted to hit out at him for his selfishness; he was only seeing things from his point of view. 'How can you even suggest such a thing!' she cried, her voice rising in her distress. 'I look upon Paul as my own, I always have. You're asking me to give away my child, do you realise that?'

Her words infuriated Derek. 'He's not your child!' he shouted out at her. 'And I wish you would realise that. So you've brought him up, you've gone without— you've scraped for him, but it doesn't alter the fact that he's not your child!'

At this point there was a polite tap on the door, and to Mary's horror the sleek dark head of Rafael Alvarados appeared round the door as if uncertain to venture further into the room. 'I do apologise,' he began, 'but I did ring the bell, and as there was no reply and the door was ajar, I took the liberty of seeking you out. It's stupid of me, I know, but I forgot to ask you for your telephone number so that I could contact you if need be. I didn't remember this until I was half way back to my office,' he added apologetically, and Mary had the feeling that he hoped to convey the fact that he had only just arrived on the scene—and what a scene!

There was an awkward pause for a moment and Mary

made a valiant attempt to cover this by swiftly introducing Derek to Rafael Alvarados, and then searching for her writing pad on which to jot her phone number down. When she had done this she handed it to him, noting that neither of the men seemed inclined to enter into desultory chat. 'It's the same prefix as for the London area,' she said breathlessly.

Rafael Alvarados thanked her and once again apologised for his intrusion, then made his departure after favouring Derek with a curt nod, leaving Mary with a ghastly impression that he had heard Derek's final outburst before he had made his presence known. He must have done, for she couldn't see how he could have avoided it—the words had been shouted out, and remembering that the front door had been ajar, there was a great possibility that any passer-by would also have heard them.

She drew a ragged breath. She couldn't blame everything on Derek, at least not the door being ajar. It had a faulty catch and had to be slammed hard, and she ought to have had it seen to ages ago. She swallowed hastily. There was nothing she could do about it now— at least not that part of it, but there was plenty she could do where Derek was concerned.

As she entered the sitting room her weary glance met Derek's shamefaced one. 'I'm sorry, Mary,' he said sheepishly. 'I lost my temper.' He took a deep breath. 'You know we've got to face this sooner or later, and now is as good a time as any. It's not often I get a chance to talk to you without the boy demanding your attention. You know what I mean,' he added. 'As a matter of fact,' he went on casually, 'I've talked this over with Mother, and we both agree that it would be better if Paul went to boarding school.'

Mary's eyes held a positive glint at this—it really was the last straw! 'Out of your way, you mean?' she asked slowly but dangerously.

There was an answering glint in Derek's eyes. 'If you put it like that, yes,' he answered coldly. 'It's not been easy for me, you know. He quite purposely flouts my orders. It's not as if I haven't tried,' he went on, hardening his jaw at the thought. 'The plain fact is, we don't get on.'

'And you think it's all Paul's fault, do you?' she asked quietly.

'Of course it is,' he replied irritably. 'I've done my best.'

'I don't think you have, Derek,' she replied coldly. 'You do know half the trouble is jealousy, don't you? Paul's jealous of you, and you're jealous of him.'

'Nonsense!' said Derek huffily. 'Whatever gave you that idea? No, he's just a spoilt brat. He's probably jealous of me, all right. Look at the way he positively haunts you when I'm around.'

But he couldn't be jealous of Paul, Mary thought wearily, he wasn't going to admit to that. Everything was going to be Paul's fault no matter what happened. It was hardly a basis for a happy marriage, was it? she thought. She slowly took the ring off the third finger of her left hand and handed it to Derek. 'I ought to have done this a long time ago,' she said quietly.

He stared at the ring and then back at her. His face was white and set. 'Do you realise what you're doing?' he asked almost incredulously.

Mary nodded. 'I know what I'm doing, Derek. I think it's best for both of us.'

'If that's the way you want it,' he said, in a vicious voice that she had not heard before, 'so be it! However,' he added pompously, 'when you come down to earth, and realise that it's your life you're living and not that brat's, perhaps we might take things up again. It's entirely up to you.'

Mary had nothing more to add and she stared down at the carpet. A moment later she heard the front door slam.

CHAPTER THREE

NINE days later Mary found herself and Paul installed in the Alvarados household. The journey over had been uneventful, if a little uncomfortable on Mary's part, for Rafael Alvarados's manner had been studiously polite, yet somehow forbidding.

That he had overheard Derek's furious outburst the evening he had called at her home was now a foregone conclusion. She knew exactly what he thought of her, and in all honesty she had to admit that if she had been in his place she, too, would have had grave doubts as to the integrity of the person involved in such machinations. She had quite blatantly lied to him about her relationship to Paul, and the fact that her motive had been an altruistic one would not make the slightest difference to him, even if he was presented with the explanation for her duplicity.

She was made to feel an interloper—a hanger-on, whose company he would have to put up with as a necessary evil, and she was as relieved as he must have been when they finally arrived at their destination.

However, Mary was able to salvage one crumb of comfort from this unhappy state of affairs, and that was that she would not have the distasteful task of lying to Enrique's father. She could now tell the truth and be done with falsehood. If the need ever arose for her to defend her earlier action in lying to Rafael Alvarados, she would apologise and explain why she had acted as she had, and hope that Rafael had been right when he had said that Enrique and his father were much alike in temperament, for if it were so, then she would be forgiven, she was sure of it.

The villa lay on the outskirts of Seville, in its own grounds, and was ample proof of the wealth of the Alvarados family. After taking a cold shower and changing into a cool cotton dress, Mary then made sure that Paul looked presentable for his introduction to his grandfather, and waited for the summons to be given to be ushered into his presence.

Her stomach churned over at the thought as she recalled Rafael Alvarados's words before placing them in the hands of an extremely dour-looking woman servant dressed entirely in black. 'My father is a late riser, but I have no doubt that he will receive you as soon as possible.'

Mary had felt a spurt of annoyance at the time. Anyone would think they were being entertained by Royalty, and she had a feeling that was just the impression he was trying to create, underlining his earlier haughty attitude towards her, and in a sense warning her to watch her step where his father was concerned. He might just as well have said, 'I shall be watching you. I don't trust you.'

Mary gave a small moue at the thought. It wasn't exactly a good basis on which to start a friendship, more like the beginning of an all-out war! It was a pity that Paul's presence had prevented a confrontation between them, for she would have liked to have been given the chance to explain why she had misled him. She gave a small sigh. Some time in the future perhaps an opportunity would present itself; in the meantime she would have to put up with his unspoken censure.

She watched Paul wandering restlessly around her

room, and was pleased that they had had the fore-
thought to give them connecting rooms so that he
would not feel lost in this large rambling residence.
He had now stopped before the shuttered window and
was attempting to open the shutters. 'No, Paul,' she
said quickly, 'it's too hot, dear. You'll have a chance
to explore the grounds after you've seen your grandfather—come and sit down for a moment.'

'I'm not too hot,' he complained lightly, and then as
a thought struck him he turned to her with wide eyes.
'Think they've a swimming pool, Mum?' he asked.

Mary gave a wry smile; from what she had seen so
far of the grounds surrounding the villa, she thought
it a likely possibility. 'I don't know, dear,' she replied,
'but no doubt you'll soon find out.'

He swished his arms about imitating a swimming
stroke. 'I'm better than Mike,' he announced proudly.
'He sinks.'

To Mary's relief there was a tap on the door, and the
woman who had shown them to their rooms entered
and told Mary in stilted English that their presence
was requested in the drawing room, and would they
please follow her.

As Mary, with Paul's hand tucked tightly into hers,
followed the tall gaunt woman down various twisting
corridors, the floors of which appeared to be of some
marble-like substance that was cool under their san-
dalled feet, she felt the same apprehension for the
future flow over her. If they made an all-out effort to
wrench Paul from her what chance did she stand of
preventing it against the weight of such wealth? What
could she offer him apart from love? The thought made
her turn pale and gave her lovely grey eyes a haunted
look.

The same haunted look was in her eyes as they entered the room indicated by the servant, and the first person Mary saw was Rafael Alvarados who stood by the wide french windows at the end of the large room and turned at their entry, favouring her with a cold haughty look, and a swift smile at Paul. She would receive no kindness from that quarter, she thought with a swift pang of panic, and wanted to about turn and leave, not only this room, but the villa, and the Alvarados's, and catch the next flight home.

A swift indrawn breath drew her attention from the hard face of Rafael Alvarados to a man standing on her left, staring at Paul with what she could only describe as a sense of wonder. 'Enrique?' he whispered in an unsteady voice, and looked back at Rafael Alvarados. 'It's unbelievable,' he said, in the same shaky voice.

Rafael Alvarados gave his father a look that embraced both tenderness and concern, and Mary wondered if she had really witnessed such a phenomenon, or whether she had imagined it, for the next moment his features were as cold and unbending as before. She watched him come forward and gently push his father down into the chair behind him from which he had obviously risen at their entry. 'You must forgive my father for not standing, Miss Allis, he ought to be in his bed, but he has insisted on receiving you here.'

Emilio Alvarados gave a weak-sounding snort and waved a thin deeply veined hand in the air as if to dispute this.

'Father, may I present Miss Allis,' said Rafael, giving her a swift glance almost as if to remind her to keep her place, and giving her permission to offer her hand to his father.

As Mary complied, only lightly resting her hand in

the pale slim one offered, she was struck by an inexplic-
able urge to confirm Rafael Alvarados's worst suspicions by gushing out some servile platitude on the
lines of, she was so pleased to meet him, and wasn't this
a lovely house? However, she managed to control herself and gave the normal greeting of, 'How do you do?'
then gave the now shy Paul a little push forward towards the man still staring at him as if unable to take
his eyes off him.

'Say hello to your grandfather, Paul,' she ordered
gently.

Paul's hand clung tighter to hers; he was obviously
overawed by the occasion and Mary couldn't blame
him. Their surroundings alone were enough to leave
him tonguetied. It was like stepping into a showroom
of opulence. Deep velvet-covered chairs, a carpet into
which one's feet sank. Pictures in gold frames on the
walls around them, various undoubtedly valuable orna-
ments on gleaming antique furniture. At the window
where Rafael Alvarados had stood on their entry hung
velvet curtaining of a deeper green than the upholstery,
and altogether it was a little too much to take, as Mary
would have described it, at one sitting. She was bemused herself, so was able to sympathise with Paul's
feelings.

'Come now, Enrique,' ordered the deep voice of
Rafael. 'You are not shy, are you?' It was said as a challenge and had the desired effect, for Paul, after shoot-
ing his uncle a surprised indignant look, immediately
offered his small hand to his grandfather, who gave a
chuckle of pure satisfaction on noting the way he had
answered the subtle challenge and solemnly accepted
the proffered hand.

The next quarter of an hour was spent in questions

and answers, on Paul's earlier childhood what school he was attending, and memories of his father's childhood were revived.

During all this time Mary saw that Rafael Alvarados kept a strict eye on his father, making certain that he did not overtire himself, and called a halt to proceedings when his father leant back in his chair for a few moments. 'If you insist on dining with us this evening,' he reminded him, 'then you must rest this afternoon.' On his father's unwillingness to comply with this suggestion, he remonstrated gently, 'Come now, you know that I am right, Father. I am sure Miss Allis would welcome a rest, too. As for Enrique,' he looked at Paul, 'I shall take him on a tour of the grounds.'

Paul's delighted grin proved that this suggestion was a welcome one. He had looked longingly out of the window several times during their discourse with his grandfather, and Mary half expected him to ask his uncle whether they had a swimming pool, for she could see he had some question he wanted answering, but whatever it was, he evidently decided to bide his time for a while.

When Emilio Alvarados had taken his leave of them, apologising to Mary for the necessity of having to take a rest before dinner, Rafael Alvarados turned to Paul with an abrupt, 'Ready, Enrique?' and walked towards the french windows that were slightly ajar and pushing them open walked out into the garden beyond, not once glancing back to see if Paul was following him. To Mary's surprise he did follow him; he was too intent on exploring his surroundings to give one thought to Mary, who watched them go with an odd sensation of being abandoned. If this was a taste of what was to come, then she wasn't going to enjoy the visit one little bit.

She made her way back to her room, only once losing her way, and being redirected by a young-looking maid she met in a corridor. The girl had spoken English, as had all the occupants of the villa, and Mary felt a spurt of pride in the knowledge that she had persevered with Spanish, and could hold a reasonably intelligent conversation in that language. Not that she had had any opportunity as yet to do so, but there might come a time when she would be grateful for the knowledge.

On entering her room she felt suddenly weary and lay down on her bed. The siesta was a must in this draining heat, and she wondered why Emilio Alvarados had not moved out to the cooler mountain areas for the summer season, as she had once read that the wealthier families did. She closed her eyes. Of course this was his home and in all probability he did not feel the heat as she did, but in spite of the efficient air-cooling system and the cool tiled floors, she felt as if she were in an oven that someone had forgotten to switch off.

As tired as she was, she did not sleep, but lay thinking about the Alvarados family, and how different their background was from hers and Paul's. Rafael Alvarados had spoken the truth when he had told her of his father's attachment to his younger son. His eyes had scarcely left Paul's face the whole time he was with them, and as ill as he obviously was she had sensed his happy animation and his inward annoyance at his weakness that forced him to retire back to his bed.

While he had been studying Paul, Mary had had ample chance to study him. It could not be said that either of his sons had taken after him in looks and certainly not in height, for Emilio Alvarados was only a inch or so taller than Mary's five feet six.

She tried to recall Enrique's height, and that he had appeared tall, but when she thought of Sheila's diminutive five feet four, she realised that in all probability he had not been a great deal taller than his father. It appeared she had confused Enrique's height with his brother Rafael, who at six foot plus towered over them all—in more ways than one, she thought darkly, as she remembered the way he had swept Paul off without seeking either her permission or her company.

Without doubt she had an enemy there, but as she thought of Emilio Alvarados she had a feeling that in him at least she would find a friend. Instinctively, she felt that he was a kindly man who would not condemn her as his son had done. His gentle expression and the deep lines across his high forehead and around his mouth told a story of suffering, physical as well as mental, and Mary wanted to ease that suffering, and in this she was in complete concord with Rafael Alvarados, if in nothing else.

Paul arrived back, but only to tell her that Uncle Rafael was taking him out to the vineyards, and that they would not be back until six. He was not asking for her permission, Mary noticed, but telling her what Rafael had told him to tell her, and she felt a spurt of annoyance at Rafael's high-handed action and very nearly said that she would go too, but held her tongue and told him to behave himself, and not ask too many questions and make a nuisance of himself, at which he replied indignantly, 'Uncle Rafael told me to ask questions!' and Mary felt that she had been well and truly put in her place!

An hour later she received another summons from Emilio Alvarados, and this time she was taken to his rooms and found him propped up in bed.

'My apologies for receiving you like this,' he said gravely, as soon as the woman servant who had escorted Mary to the room left. 'I am forced to obey my son's ruling and take the allotted rest period before we dine this evening.' He gave her an anxious look. 'I hope you have had sufficient rest yourself?' he asked solicitously.

'Ample, thank you,' replied Mary with a tentative smile. 'I'm not in the habit of resting in the afternoon, you know, but here ...' She bit her lip in vexation. Another second and she would have told him how the heat had affected her, and she didn't want to sound complaining.

He smiled at her, and indicated a chair by his bed-side. 'Come and sit down, Mary—I may call you Mary, mayn't I?'

'Of course,' answered Mary swiftly, 'I would prefer you to.'

He waited until she had settled herself in the chair, then said, 'It's the heat, that's what you were going to say, wasn't it?'

Mary's candid eyes met his twinkling ones. 'It's just that I'm not used to it,' she explained haltingly. 'I expect I shall get used to it,' she added hopefully.

He nodded understandingly. 'I can only apologise again,' he said. 'It was not the best time of year for your visit.' He looked towards his bedroom window, shuttered, as were Mary's windows, against the glare of the sun. 'There was a time when the family moved to what we used to call "our mountain retreat".' He gave an abrupt sigh and looked back towards her. 'It was a long time ago, though. Now there is only myself, and it hardly seems worth the effort.'

Mary did not know what to say. It must have been

lonely for him with his only surviving son living, it appeared, away from home. No matter what nationality, that very precious link that can only be formed by family was an essential part of living.

'Have you a family, Mary?' he asked suddenly, cutting into her thoughts.

Mary told him how when she was ten, and Sheila nine, they were placed in an orphanage. Their father had left their mother, and she had been unable to cope. On seeing the look of consternation this news brought her companion, she hastily said, 'Oh, it was the best thing that could have happened to us. We were much happier there than at home where we weren't wanted. At least we were together, and we stayed together. There was no question of either of us being adopted.'

Her eyes settled on the rich silk counterpane on his bed. 'We rarely saw our mother, only when she was impelled by some spark of conscience would she make the effort to visit. Then she stopped coming altogether.' Her fine eyes met his sympathetic ones. 'We rather thought she'd met someone else and hadn't told them that she had two daughters.' She shrugged lightly. 'Well, time went by, and eventually we were told that she had died, it didn't mean anything to us, she had become only a dim memory by then.'

'And that was why you kept the boy,' said Emilio Alvarados softly, 'although it couldn't have been easy for you when you lost your sister.'

Mary flung him a quick surprised look. In those few words he had told her that he knew that she was not Paul's mother, and more than this, he knew that Sheila had died. Rafael Alvarados, it appeared, had been very busy, and had obviously clarified the position for his father. As for the reason why she had kept Paul, he was partially right, yet not wholly so. 'Because we were brought up in an orphanage, you mean?' she queried slowly, then carried on before he could reply, 'I can't honestly say that our upbringing had anything to do with it. As I have said, we were happy, but it was more than that; I loved my sister, Señor Alvarados, and when I lost her Paul was all I had left. I loved him because he was part of her.' She fell silent. How do you explain things like that?

'When did she die, Mary?' he asked gently. 'At the boy's birth?'

Mary shook her head. 'When Paul was six months old, a railway accident,' she replied quietly. There was so much more she wanted to say, such as how from that moment on Paul had regarded her as his mother, and would always do so, and why she had not felt it necessary to tell Paul the truth. She hesitated and looked back at the man who sat watching her, and there was something in his dark eyes that gave her encouragement. 'Señor Alvarados——' she began.

'Don Emilio,' he broke in with a wisp of an apologetic smile.

Mary coloured. 'I do beg your pardon,' she apologised, 'but your son didn't ...' she broke off in confusion. Wretched man! he hadn't thought it necessary to introduce his father to her, only her to him, as if that was all that mattered, and in his eyes it was. She was only there on sufferance.

He raised his hand in what was becoming a familiar gesture to Mary. 'I apologise for my son's lack of manners,' he said, somewhat sorrowfully, and gazed down at his white slim hand on the counterpane. 'Rafael has always been a law unto himself. Do not let his forbidding manner intimidate you. I can assure you that he improves upon acquaintance. His shoulders are broad, and he has carried our little empire on them for more years than I care to remember.'

Mary said nothing, as she had no wish to contradict Don Emilio on his optimistic view of her relationship with his son improving in time, for she doubted if either of them had got that much time to spare, or indeed the wish to attain such a happy state.

To her relief he changed the conversation abruptly and asked, 'You have no objection to my calling ... er ... Paul by what I learnt from my son as his first name, Enrique?'

Mary shook her head but swallowed a lump that had arisen in her throat. This was just the beginning. She, too, would have to learn to call him Enrique, even though she would always think of him as Paul.

As if sensing her feelings, Don Emilio again changed the subject and asked her about her work. 'My son told me that you are a teacher. Are you happy in this work?'

Mary blinked a little at this abrupt change of subject and gave the question a little thought. If she answered honestly she would say that she had been perfectly happy in her present situation until a change of headship had occurred; since then she had considered seeking another post, even though this would have meant her travelling quite a distance from her home, and would have brought her a few worries about leaving Paul on his own until her return. However, this was a situation yet to be resolved, and as yet she had pushed the matter aside in the vain hope perhaps that things would work out. She compromised by answering slowly, 'It's the only work I want to do,' and left it at that.

Her slight hesitation did not go unnoticed by Don Emilio. 'But you are not entirely happy in your present job?' he persisted gently.

Mary sighed inwardly. How perceptive the man was, and in that respect it appeared Rafael took after him. 'Well,' she replied hesitantly, 'I was thinking of looking for another post—in another school, that is,' and that was as far as she would go.

The news pleased Don Emilio, who nodded to himself for a second or so before saying, 'In that case, the question I am about to ask you will perhaps receive a favourable hearing.' He leant forward towards her, his dark heavy-lidded eyes staring into hers as if to compel her attention, again reminding her of Rafael, who had the same way of capturing his audience's attention, only Rafael's effect was more devastating on the senses and more mesmerising. 'I want you to seriously consider staying here with Enrique,' he said abruptly.

Mary's eyes registered the shock his words had given her. 'I don't—I didn't——' she began, then fell silent, unable to express her thoughts coherently.

'Please!' entreated Don Emilio earnestly. 'Do not try to give me an answer yet. Take your time; I have no wish to extract a promise from you that you will later regret giving.' He looked away from the still stupefied Mary and gave his attention to the velvet cuff of his dressing gown. 'I do, however, wish you to take certain things into consideration, the foremost being that I intend to make provision for Enrique's future, inasmuch as he will in due course of time inherit half the Alvarados estate as his father would have done, had he lived.'

This was exactly what Mary had feared would be the outcome of their visit, and she didn't know why she felt so stunned. It was the timing, perhaps; it had come much earlier than she had anticipated. Don Emilio,

like his son, believed in laying his cards upon the table,
and what a hand it was, a royal flush indeed!

Her thoughts were echoed in her wide eyes as she
met his searching ones. 'Do not look so lost, my child,'
he said gently. 'I do not intend to snatch Enrique from
you. He needs you, as I need him.' The last words were
said in a low voice and held a pleading note in them
that Mary found hard to ignore.

She looked down at her hands clasped tightly in her
lap. Did he know what he was asking of her? That she
should leave her home and settle in a foreign land—
just like that? What if she had still been engaged to
Derek?

'I am exceedingly stupid!' Don Emilio exclaimed,
after the short pregnant silence that had fallen after his
last words. 'You are perhaps attached to someone?' he
asked gently.

Mary knew what he meant. So the redoubtable
Rafael had omitted to tell him that she was engaged—
or had been. This did not surprise her; he was running
true to form. He was simply not interested in her, only
Paul. She could, of course, lie and say yes, there was
someone, and perhaps gain a little breathing space,
but she was done with lying. Her grey eyes met the
probing ones of Don Emilio as she answered slowly,
'No, there is no one.'

'Well, we shall discuss it no more for the time being,'
he replied in a voice that showed his satisfaction at this
state of affairs. 'Tomorrow I will get Rafael to show
you over the estate.'

This, Mary realised, was the end of the interview—
she couldn't call it anything else, although Don Emilio
had done his best not to make it appear so. As she
reached the door he said in a light almost teasing voice,

'October will suit you better, Mary. The sun still shines, but without such ferocity.'

Mary's thoughts hovered between exasperation and righteous indignation. He had taken her acceptance of his offer as a natural conclusion in spite of his earlier direction that she should give the matter some thought. She didn't know about Paul's father, but his uncle, she thought darkly, most certainly took after his father— neither, it appeared, was averse to using blockbusting tactics to gain their objective!

By the time she was back in her room she felt as if she had been pushed off the edge of a mountain, and was now floating down to what she hoped would be a soft landing, but she was by no means sure. She was getting a little tired of having her mind made up for her by the formidable Alvarados family. She liked Don Emilio, and she wanted to help him, but not at the expense of her and Paul's happiness.

A glance at her watch told her that it was about time Paul came back, and she wondered if she ought to go down to the kitchen to arrange his supper for him. Dinner, she had learnt, would be at eight-thirty, and much too late for Paul's attendance.

She walked over to the window and opened the shutters to let what breeze there might be into the room. The heat of the day had somewhat lessened, and she looked forward to the evening coolness in the hope of getting some alleviation from the sick headache that was beginning to make itself felt at the back of her temples.

The vista that met her eyes was one of landscaped beauty; the gardens sloped down from the villa into the distance. Away on her right she caught the glistening rays of a fountain spray that rose high into the air,

but the shrubs surrounding it effectively curtailed
closer inspection. She would have to find that fountain,
and if it were not for Paul's imminent arrival back
from the vineyards she would have gone in search of it
right then, for she couldn't imagine anything nicer than
to stand close to that sparkling cascade of water and
feel the cool spray on her upturned face.

When Paul eventually returned to her he had had
supper, and though Mary's head was by now throbbing
with an intensity that made her want to lie down and
seek release in sleep, she again felt that surge of resent-
ment against Rafael Alvarados, who had thoughtfully
seen to Paul's welfare in the catering line, and given
orders to that effect.

'Uncle Rafael showed me some horses, Mum,' he
said, his dark eyes sparkling in memory. 'And he said
he'll teach me to ride,' and then added practically in
the same breath, 'There's a pony there just right for me,
he's all black with a white streak down his nose. Uncle
Rafael says——'

By the time Mary had packed him off to bed, she was
heartily sick of what his Uncle Rafael had said, or
hadn't said! As for what Paul had thought of the vineyards—well, it appeared that once he had seen the
horses, all else had been driven from his mind, and
Mary would have to wait to see them for herself the
following day.

As there was still an hour and a half to go before
dinner, she took advantage of the free time by taking
some aspirin and the rest she so badly needed. Heat
could be wearying, quite apart from the astounding
result of her interview with Don Emilio and its attendant problems, the answers to which she would have
to have ready in the not too distant future. It would

be cowardly of her to let things slide and give him the impression that he had won the day. On the other hand, she could hardly seek another interview with him at this early stage and bluntly tell him that there was no possibility of her complying with his suggestion that she and Paul should take up permanent residence in Spain.

It was odd, she thought, how Don Emilio had seized on her slight hesitation when she had spoken about her job. He would be even more certain of his ground and would be sure to press home his advantage had he known that Mary could easily walk out of the job without fear of recrimination, or of bad references, since there happened to be someone waiting on the sidelines to step into her shoes. When this someone happened to be the headmaster's wife, who had been waiting for just such an opportunity since her husband had been granted the headship, Mary's dilemma was clear.

The fact that it was a small private school made her position less tenable than it might otherwise have been. Mary knew that it was only a question of time before she was ousted, and the insecurity of her position had been a source of private worry to her for some time now. Had there been a school within reasonable distance of her home, she would have gracefully paved the way for her determined antagonist, but quite apart from the fact that no such school existed within fifteen miles of her home, there was no guarantee that there would be a job available for her. It was a true but sad fact of the times that jobs were scarce, hence the pressure being applied by her opponent.

She then thought of what Don Emilio had said about Paul inheriting the Alvarados estates, and this made her think of Rafael Alvarados. He had known this, of course, indeed he had hinted at such a possibility, yet he was still a comparatively young man and able to have children of his own who would surely expect to inherit the estate, particularly as their father was the eldest son.

Her smooth forehead creased as she tried to recall something he had said on their first meeting, since she was sure that it had something to do with this strange state of affairs. Then she had it: he had said something about disappointing his father. So that was it—he had not married! And by all accounts had no intention of so doing, therefore providing no heirs to the estate.

Her frown deepened as she considered this salient fact. Was he a woman-hater? She shook her head at this; he mightn't care for her, but she was sure that as fastidious as he was, he would be as aware of any attractive woman as any other man would be. Aware, she thought, but shut off from the light flirtatious invitations to dalliance that a man who was as attractive to the opposite sex as he was would be bound to receive from more intrepid females. With his height, his proud bearing, and his handsome latin looks, he automatically commanded attention. Mary had not failed to notice this on the journey over, nor the covert, almost envious looks she had caught on the faces of their fellow passengers, particularly the female ones.

On this thought she gave a wry smile. They must have wondered what he was doing in the company of such a dull, plain-looking woman, and must have come to the conclusion that she was a hired hand employed to look after the child whose comfort he was at pains to achieve. One look at him and then at Paul would have proclaimed the fact that they were related, and in all probability they had reached the same conclusion as Mary herself had on her first acquaintance with Rafael, that Paul was his son.

Why hadn't he married? she asked herself. Had he loved and lost? Would no other woman come up to his high standards? She gave another tiny shake of the head; she simply couldn't see him as the forlorn lover standing aside with bowed head as the woman he loved married someone else. He would be more likely to lay a siege to her until he had obtained his heart's desire, ruthlessly cutting down any opposition to his goal!

On this thought she fell into a deep dreamless sleep.

CHAPTER FOUR

MARY was awoken by the sound of a deep-sounding gong, and she lay for a moment or two wondering why someone should be sounding a gong. She did not possess one, so how could—— Then realisation hit her that she was not at home but in the Alvarados household.

She sat up quickly and stared at her watch, then gave a horrified gasp and shook it as if in disbelief. It simply couldn't be eight-twenty; dinner was at eight-thirty!

She hadn't time to work out how she had managed to sleep for that length of time—in the early evening, too, —something she had never done before. One look at her crumpled dress told her that she would have to find something else to wear, and in frantic haste she searched for another dress, not really caring whether it was suitable or not just as long as it was presentable, and took the first one that came to hand. This was a white linen pinafore-styled dress, with a square neck, and was sleeveless.

There was no time to linger over her toilet either, and she ran a quick comb through her hair. With three minutes to spare she rushed out of her room and went in search of the dining room.

Her fear that she might not find the dining room was allayed by the appearance of a maid who was hovering at the bottom of the staircase obviously waiting for Mary's arrival, and she conducted her to the dining room.

Flushed and slightly embarrassed, Mary walked into the room where her hosts awaited her, and her embarrassment heightened when she saw that both the men were impeccably dressed in evening wear, Don Emilio favouring a close-fitting jacket and frilled shirt front, while his son Rafael looked resplendent in the more conventional Western-styled suit with a plain but expensive white silk shirt.

She felt bad enough without encountering Rafael's disparaging eyes. 'I do apologise,' she began hesitantly, 'I didn't know ...' although she ought to have known that they would have dressed for dinner, she told herself disparagingly, and if she hadn't overslept, no doubt the idea would have occurred to her; as it was, she had only just been able to make her appearance at the appointed time.

'Please,' soothed Don Emilio, as he ushered her to her seat at the beautifully polished table now set with gleaming silver and sparkling glasses, 'don't distress yourself. I must say that white becomes you.'

Mary sat down and felt a surge of gratitude towards Don Emilio, and the smile she gave him clearly spoke her thoughts, but her smile froze on her lips when she found that she was placed opposite Rafael Alvarados, with Don Emilio at the head of the large table. She only needed to spill her soup or use the wrong cutlery and her disgrace would be complete, she told herself miserably, and she fervently wished that Rafael Alvarados could find some reason for absenting himself from the villa until their departure. It was obvious that he did not spend much time at his home in Seville being too busy running the business side of affairs, as his father had intimated.

The food, she noticed, with another little spurt of

gratitude towards Don Emilio, was more on the lines
of an English meal, and she was sure that this consideration was due to his intervention, since she knew
that the Spaniards were fond of spicy concoctions. She
had tasted the faintest suggestion of garlic in the main
course and surmised that the idea was to gently break
her into the seasoned culinary arts of the household
kitchen.

Quite apart from the fact that she had little appetite,
the forbidding presence of the man opposite her completely erased any hope that she would enjoy the dinner, in spite of Don Emilio's determined efforts to put
her at her ease. By the time the dinner had ended
Mary was certain of one thing, and that was that if
Rafael Alvarados intended to make a long stay at home,
wild horses would not prevent her from leaving at the
earliest given opportunity!

She was very sorry to disappoint Don Emilio, but
there were limits, and she had no intention of leaving
Paul with the Alvarados family, inheritance or no inheritance! she thought as she accepted a delicately en-
graved cup and saucer from Rafael, when they had retired to the *salón* for coffee.

The following hour seemed to drag for Mary, although Don Emilio kept her busy with questions on
one topic or another, with little or no help from his son,
who appeared to be in a world of his own and only
replied to direct questions put to him by his father in
an abortive effort to draw him into whatever subject
they were discussing.

The only reason for his continued presence during
that time, Mary discovered, was to keep an eye on his
father and make certain that he did not overtire himself, and she knew a surge of relief when he called a

halt to the proceedings shortly after eleven, remarking in a light but firm voice that it was time that he retired.

There was no doubt that Don Emilio was tired, although he made a valiant effort to disguise this fact from Mary, but she saw how drawn he was and added her persuasion, saying that she, too, would shortly be going to bed.

Before he left, Don Emilio mentioned the arrangement that Rafael should take Mary on a tour of the estate, but judging from the frown this produced from Rafael, Mary assumed that he had not been advised of this. 'I'm sorry, Father,' he said in clipped tones, 'but you must have forgotten that I am due to see the overseer about that extra shipment we require, and I had planned,' he added autocratically, 'to spend most of the day there. There would not be a great deal for Miss Allis to see apart from the wine vats and the bottling operations.' He turned an icy eye on Mary. 'I'm sure you will forgive me for not complying with my father's suggestion. Had I known of the arrangement ...'

Mary hastily intervened here; she no more wanted his company than he wanted hers, and if he had been going to say that he might have been able to make other arrangements, she knew it would have been a downright lie. As if he would allow someone like her to forestall his plans! 'Please, don't worry about it,' she said sweetly, although her sparkling eyes belied her tone, 'there'll be plenty of time for me to see the estate— Paul can show me around.'

'I had thought of taking Enrique with me,' answered Rafael, swiftly answering the unspoken challenge in Mary's eyes. He looked back at his father standing watching this little interchange with a mixture of exasperation and annoyance at his son's deliberately provocative attitude towards Mary. 'Pedro's son is much the same age as Enrique, I thought perhaps they should get acquainted.'

It appeared to be a suggestion put to his father for his approval at which Don Emilio gave a shrug that plainly said, 'You will do as you want, as usual', but there was something in the look that he gave his son that told Mary that he was displeased with him, then he looked back at Mary in an apologetic manner.

The ball, it appeared, was in Mary's court, and she wanted to throw it out of play with the contempt that she felt at having been put in such a position. However, for Don Emilio's sake, she decided to give way and with her head held high, she said mildly, 'Very well; it will be nice for Paul to meet someone of his own age,' fervently wanting to add, 'Game, set and match to Rafael Alvarados!'

The following morning Paul was collected shortly after eight by the same elderly servant who appeared to be a cross between a housekeeper and a personal attendant, and to Mary's surprise he made no objection at being whisked out of her room where he had gone to join her an hour earlier, and bundled into the adjoining bathroom. A still sleepy Mary had lain listening to the splashing sound of activity emanating from the bathroom, interspersed with Paul's high childish queries on this and that, not a bit put out, Mary thought with a sense of wonder, at the fact that a stranger was seeing to his ablutions. She could hear the old woman's deep voice answering him in English, but every now and again would break into her native tongue, in what sounded like light scolding alternated with endearments.

Ten minutes later a well scrubbed and anxious to

be off Paul presented himself for Mary's inspection before being taken down to breakfast, and with a happy, 'Uncle Rafael is going to teach me to ride,' he dashed out of the room as if afraid to be late for this very important occasion, leaving Mary to her own devices.

She had just finished dressing when she heard the sound of horse's hoofs close by and opened the window shutters and looked out. The sight that met her eyes made her hold her breath in a wonderment that was tinged with sadness that her sister was not there to witness the sight of her son sitting proudly in front of the stiffly erect figure of Rafael Alvarados seated on a magnificent black stallion. A hat had been found for him, Mary saw, not unlike the sombrero type of hat worn by his uncle.

As Mary's eyes lingered on them taking in again the amazing likeness between uncle and nephew, they both glanced up at her window as if sensing her surveillance, and she stepped back quickly out of sight feeling as if she had been caught spying on them—and that was ridiculous, she told herself crossly. Why shouldn't she be waiting to see them off? It was a natural thing for any mother to do, wasn't it?

The memory of those two upturned faces remained with her for the rest of the morning, Paul's hopeful one, eager to show off, and Rafael's haughty one that clearly said, 'Go about your business, woman, the boy is where he belongs, and the sooner you realise it the better.'

Mary ate a solitary breakfast laid out on the terrace adjoining the dining room, and she wondered if Don Emilio would request her presence that morning, or whether she would be left to amuse herself. The latter was the most agreeable to her in her present mood that was one of infinite sadness, for she knew that she had no choice but to do exactly as Don Emilio had asked her to do and stay in Seville.

It was Paul that mattered, not her, and she knew now that her fears that he would be unhappy were groundless, since it would be she who would make him unhappy should she insist on their returning to England. Not that that would make any difference now to him, he would go where she went because they belonged to each other, but the time would come when he would have to learn that she had deliberately turned her back on his people—not only that, but his inheritance.

She stared ahead of her at the sweeping lawns and immaculate flower borders on which sprinklers were being trained before the sun's fierce heat penetrated through. Of course they could go back home, and maybe arrange to visit again in the not too distant future, she thought musingly, but was that fair? What would Paul remember of his grandfather? Wouldn't it be harder each time? Links made, then severed, and Paul would find himself torn between two homes.

If the question were put to him at this moment in time whether he wanted to stay here or go back, Mary knew which he would choose. It wasn't only the excitement of discovery, or of the fact that he was going to learn to ride. It went much deeper than that. There was a saying, she thought, that summed it up nicely, and that was 'to the manner born'. He had instinctively known that he belonged here. Look at the way that he had accepted the old servant's administrations that morning. The old Paul would have had no truck with such goings on and would have been highly indignant, not to mention furious, at what he considered an intrusion on his privacy. Mary was in no doubt that the old retainer had been Rafael's and Enrique's nurse all those years ago, and intended to carry on in the same capacity with Enrique's son.

Last but not least was the undeniable fact that Sheila would have wanted her son to live in the environment in which he belonged. Mary gave a deep sigh. As for herself, it wasn't going to be so easy; she couldn't see herself as a lady of leisure for one thing, and she certainly couldn't see an amicable relationship blossoming between herself and Rafael Alvarados for another. All she could hope for at that moment was that he would take himself off in the near future and attend to the Alvarados's business ties in London where apparently he had been working when Mary had literally bumped into him.

As for the future, perhaps she could get herself a job teaching English? At this thought she frowned, and then slowly shook her head. That would not do at all, for quite apart from what she was sure would be Rafael Alvarados's opinion on such a move since his attitude, she was certain, would be one of, 'a mother's place was in the home', particularly as from his point of view there would be no need for her to exert herself in this direction, there was Don Emilio to consider, and his pride, she was also sure, would not countenance her seeking work of any description.

Having reached that conclusion Mary saw no point in pursuing that train of thought; she was on that plane again suspended in mid-air and waiting to alight at some unknown destination. The thought that Rafael Alvarados was the pilot of the plane gave her little comfort. In a sense, she mused, even Don Emilio was a passenger, as was Paul, and neither of them had any control over the chosen route, and it was a chilling thought. At least Don Emilio and Paul had nothing to fear, but the same could not be said of her position. She would be dropped off at the first available point, be it desert or jungle, and left to fend for herself.

In spite of the heat now beginning to make itself felt Mary shivered, and gave herself a mental shake. She was delving into the realms of fantasy, and surely things were not as bad as all that. Perhaps, as Don Emilio had said, their acquaintance would improve in time, however dim the prospect appeared to be right then.

It was at this point that she received a message from Don Emilio to the effect that he would be gratified if she would take lunch with him at midday, and she sent back her thanks and acceptance.

As she now had the rest of the morning at her disposal, her thoughts turned towards the fountain that she had seen from her bedroom window, and she went in search of it.

She eventually found it, as she had noticed earlier, behind a screen of high shrubbery that formed a dark green shaded area for its setting. The area directly around the fountain was paved in pastel-tinted tiles of a blue and rose colouring, and directly behind the fountain and shaded by the tall shrubbery was a garden seat that Mary settled herself down on, and watched the cascade of water that spouted out in a high plume of sparkling droplets from a torch held high by a marble figurine carved in the classical style.

She sat entranced, almost feeling the light spray of the water as it fell in curtainlike droplets over the still and beautifully carved figure.

It was a scene that she felt that she would never tire of, and she was quite content to stay there for as long as time permitted, but after a while her thoughts returned to her earlier ruminations on the future. There would be a lot she would have to do now that she had made her mind up about staying. She would have to write to the school and send in her notice. No problem there, she thought wryly, but plenty of jubilation on a certain person's part!

Of course, she would have to go back and see to the packing at home, and what was she to do about the house? What if things didn't work out? Where would she be then? Accommodation was not all that easy to find, but if Paul was not going to return with her she would not want a place as large as their present home. Besides, she bit her lower lip, she could not envisage herself living there without him; it would bring back too many memories.

She felt suddenly breathless as she realised where her thoughts were taking her. It was as if she knew what was going to happen. Paul would stay—and she would go. Not as yet, of course, but at some time in the future. She would have to face up to that fact sooner or later. She had no right to hold on to him any longer than was necessary. Her influence on him would lessen in time, and this was how it should be. It was a lesson that every mother had to learn—how to let go, and Mary had no intention of clinging on to the bitter end. Her hands clenched into small fists by her side. When that time came she would tell Paul that she was not his mother but his aunt, and by that time he would be so immersed in his family background that it would not cause him any heartache.

As if to avert the inevitable, Mary decided not to do anything about the problem of the house until it was really necessary. If she gave up the lease, she would have to find somewhere to store their furniture, and that would be costly. Although, she thought ironically, she would only have to mention this to Don Emilio and he would undoubtedly offer to cover this expense for her, and she did not want this to happen.

This was not the only reason why she decided to leave things in abeyance. She might not have a job when she got back, but at least she would have somewhere to live while she sorted herself out. When she did manage to get a job she would probably find a flat for herself near her work, perhaps even be able to find a post that provided living-in accommodation with it.

Beyond that, she refused to contemplate. It was going to be hard for her to start again, to learn to think singularly and not plurally—not to metion the loneliness that this state of being was likely to bring about.

She got up abruptly and moved away from the fountain, as if by this action alone she could stave off the inevitable. She moved on through the landscaped gardens with a heavy heart, scarcely able to appreciate the bright vista around her.

As the time neared for her lunch appointment with Don Emilio, she made her way back to the house in a kind of semi-circle and discovered a swimming pool, and wondered if Paul had learned of its existence.

It was surrounded by the same kind of tiling as that around the fountain, and its clear pale blue coloured base was reflected in the water and looked inviting, particularly as the heat of the morning had now reached a high temperature. She ought to have remembered to bring a hat, Mary thought as she followed a paved path through an avenue of what looked like poplar trees, that provided a screen for the pool, and led directly to the back entrance of the villa.

After she had made herself presentable, she went

down to the dining room and found Don Emilio waiting for her on the patio. There was now a large parasol
over the table that gave ample protection from the
sun's fierce rays.

At her approach Don Emilio rose out of the cane
chair that he had been reclining on while he awaited
her arrival, and Mary was again reminded of the difference between father and son. She simply could not
see Rafael carrying out such precise courtesy, not where
she was concerned anyway, she thought, as she took
his hand that was held out to her in greeting.

Lunch consisted of a large dish of tempting-looking
prawns and various tiny sandwiches, filled either with
some kind of sausage, or shrimp and crayfish, which-
ever appealed to the palate. Afterwards coffee was
served, and Mary could not remember tasting such a
delicious beverage, particularly when she thought of
the concoction that steamed out of the machine that
the school had had installed, and that went by the same
name.

After enquiring after Don Emilio's health and receiving the smiling reply that he was feeling better than he
had for some time, Mary was reminded of a remark of
Rafael's in which he had intimated that his father
desperately needed a reason for his recovery and how
he was sure that his grandchild's presence would provide that reason.

It appeared to Mary as she watched the way Don
Emilio's eyes lit up at the very mention of his grandson
that Rafael's diagnosis had been correct, for already
she could see an improvement in him.

Under these circumstances it was just as well that she
had decided to accept Don Emilio's invitation to stay
with them. She did not look on it as a subtle kind of

blackmail, not now that she had met Don Emilio, for she liked him far too much to harbour any such thought.

'It will be good for Enrique to meet Juan,' commented Don Emilio, and Mary wondered if he was apologising for Rafael's high-handed action in taking him off with him that morning. 'Unfortunately we are some distance from our nearest neighbour, and Juan has had to amuse himself,' he told Mary.

Mary thought about the language problem, but supposed that children had a language of their own and would find a way of communicating with each other.

Don Emilio saw her look of uncertainty, and smiled at her. 'Juan's mother is English,' he said. 'It appears that my Enrique was not the only one with a penchant for an English rose.'

Mary's surprise showed in her eyes, and she felt an odd spurt of relief that a countrywoman of hers should be living so near. It made her feel less of an alien, and she hoped to be able to meet her in the near future.

'I will see that you make her acquaintance,' promised Don Emilio, who seemed to have the knack of picking up Mary's thoughts.

'Thank you, I would like that very much,' replied Mary, giving him a grateful smile. 'Has she lived here long?' she asked.

Don Emilio's eyes took on a bleak look as he replied, 'Since her marriage to my overseer eight years ago.' He was silent for a few seconds after this, then added, 'Juan is now six years old.'

Mary could guess at the memories this innocent question of hers had evoked and wished she had not asked it. Their marriage must have taken place shortly before Enrique's death.

She did not know what to say, but she was saved from making the attempt of thinking up another subject to take his mind off the past by Don Emilio giving himself a mental shake and favouring Mary with a wan smile. 'The Santos family have been with us for years. Pedro's father was my overseer, and his father before him. The children have grown up together through the years. Enrique used to play with Pedro when he was young. Rafael, you understand, was that much older. There was ten years between them.' He gave a deep sigh. 'It is good that Enrique's son should grow up with Juan.'

That was all he said, yet Mary knew that he had derived much satisfaction and comfort from this thought, and she was relieved when the conversation turned to other matters.

CHAPTER FIVE

An excited Paul sought out Mary shortly after six, full of the day's happenings, and for once his conversation did not centre on horses or the pony his uncle had promised him, but on his new-found friend Juan Santos.

'He's younger than me, Mum,' he said happily, as if this state of affairs pleased him. 'But he can ride,' he added a little less enthusiastically. 'He can't talk as well as I can,' he tacked on ruminatively.

'You mean he can't speak English as well as you do,' Mary corrected him gently. 'But you don't speak Spanish and he does, so you're even, aren't you?'

Paul nodded thoughtfully, then looked up at her. 'He calls his mother Madre,' he commented, and his expressive brows lifted as a thought occurred to him. 'I shall call you Madre too,' he announced solemnly.

Mary felt a tightening around her heart, but she replied evenly enough, 'Very well, dear,' and hastily piloted him into the bathroom to prepare him for bed.

'He's coming over here tomorrow,' he said, as he stifled a huge yawn.

'Oh, good,' replied Mary absently as she gathered up his clothes, wondering at the same time what facilities there were for washing there. His shirt and jeans would have to be seen to, she thought, as she noticed how grubby they were. It was then that she spotted a large rent in his shirt, a new one bought just before they came. 'Oh, Paul! How on earth did you get this tear in your shirt?' she said exasperatedly.

Scrubbing himself dry with a large towel that completely eclipsed his small figure, Paul looked over the top of the material at her and gave her an indignant look. 'Uncle Rafael and Juan call me Enrique,' he complained. 'I don't like being called Paul,' he told her with an air of hauteur. His gaze then settled on the torn shirt that she held for his attention. 'We climbed trees,' he said, as if that explained everything, which it did of course, but Mary did wish he had been a little more careful.

'I hope Juan didn't tear his clothes, too,' she commented, thinking it would hardly foster good relations between Juan's mother and herself if she thought Paul was a ruffian liable to lead her son into scrapes.

' 'Course not!' replied Paul. 'He knew the way up, didn't he? I got stuck on a branch, but I know the way now,' he ended satisfactorily, and that was the end of the matter.

As Mary tucked him up and bent to drop a kiss on his soap-scented forehead, he gave her a drowsy smile. 'Night, Madre,' he murmured sleepily, and with a contented sigh fell asleep.

As Mary looked down at the child she had watched over since his babyhood, she felt infinitely sad. In a way she had already lost him; long before she had expected to. What should have been a gradual process of growing apart had suddenly been speeded up at a rate that took her breath away

He was now Enrique, and she was Madre, and the signs of change were already showing in the small boy that she knew so well.

Her gaze lingered on his finely boned face with the wing-shaped brows, and the incredibly long eyelashes that now lay against his honeyed cheek in sleep, then moved on to his blue-black hair, fluffy now after his bath, but normally smoothed back across his forehead. 'Don't grow up like your Uncle Rafael,' she whispered fervently. 'Don't be proud and cold, but kind and considerate like your grandfather.'

Now that Enrique was asleep Mary could attend to her own affairs, and she was glad to have something to do to take her mind off her miserable musings. For one thing she had to find herself a suitable dress to wear at dinner that evening, as she had found to her discomfort the previous evening that the Alvarados's dressed for dinner, and that meant that she, too, would have to find something that would pass muster, and this was not going to be an easy task as she did not possess an evening gown. She did, however, possess two dresses that could be used in lieu, and were in fact cocktail dresses of a three-quarter length, bought for the odd special occasion when she had had to attend the annual dinner given by her employers and which she could not absent herself from since it would have caused some offence.

She took one of the dresses out of the wardrobe and held it away from her for inspection. Of the two dresses, this was her favourite. It was a soft rose-print dress with a scoop neck and long sleeves with frilled cuffs, and would certainly not disgrace her hosts' impeccable dress sense.

As her eyes lingered on the tiered skirt, Mary recalled Derek's chagrin the last time she had worn the dress simply because she had worn it before at one of his college dinners a few weeks earlier. She remembered telling him that it was highly unlikely that anyone would remember just what she had worn at that dinner and didn't he like the dress? He had replied that of course he liked the dress, but surely she could have bought herself another one. He had ended by adding a stinking remark that if she didn't spend so much on Paul she would have been able to afford to buy herself what he considered essentials, but once they were married he would see to all that.

Her lips formed a soft moue at this recollection. He had no idea just how expensive children's clothes were, and Mary had had to buy Paul a blazer at that particular time. As it was, she had had to slim her budget that month to cover that expense. Well, that was one worry she would not have to face now. She had been secretly dreading having to beg and explain in minute detail why it would have been necessary to buy Paul this or that. As for the little luxuries, such as fads of the moment that all children go through, she had very much doubted her success in pleading for those. It wouldn't, she thought sadly, have been quite so hard if Paul had been Derek's son, but he wasn't. In Derek's eyes he had been a rival for her affections and there was little chance of a better relationship resulting from their marriage.

She sighed and laid the dress down on the bed. Yes, she had done the right thing in turning him down. Even, she thought with a surprised start, if she were to return tomorrow without Paul, she had no wish to resume her earlier association with Derek. So she had not loved him—only tried to convince herself that she did. All in all she had had a lucky escape, she told herself. It appeared she ought to be grateful to Rafael Alvarados for his timely appearance on the scene just when she had run out of excuses as to why they should postpone their marriage.

A sharp tap on the door made her jump and glance at her watch. It was not time for dinner, there was an hour and a half to go yet. On opening her door she was surprised to see Rafael Alvarados standing there with a bundle of dresses over his arm, and she watched with astonishment as he swept into her room and put the dresses down on the bed. 'I think you will find these are your size,' he said crisply, adding with an offhand shrug, 'if not, you must blame Maria.'

Mary blinked and stared from him to the dresses on the bed, spread out, it seemed, for her approval, and back at Rafael again, and waited for an explanation. She had taken particular note that they were evening dresses.

He inclined his haughty head towards the dresses. 'With my father's compliments,' he said brusquely.

Mary's brows lifted; he had said 'with my father's compliments' but she was certain that Don Emilio would never have embarrassed her with such a gesture. This was Rafael's way of making sure that she did not disgrace the family by making the same mistake as she had made last night. 'Please thank him for me,' she said stiffly as she felt a surge of cold fury building up inside her. 'Although I'm afraid I shall have no use for them.'

Rafael's eyes narrowed at this simple statement and she knew that he was furious and was having a hard time controlling his temper.

'I apologise again for not realising that you would dress for dinner,' she went on calmly. 'I do possess a few dresses that would pass muster for evening wear.' She glanced back at the dresses on the bed. 'Not quite as elegant as those, I admit, but quite suitable, I assure you.'

She watched his finely moulded lips tighten and could guess at the thoughts going on behind that cold reserve of his. Suitable for her but not for the Alvarados family. He shrugged his powerful shoulders. 'As you wish,' he said curtly. 'We have guests this evening.' His cold eyes met hers. 'You wouldn't want to disappoint my father, would you.'

It was not a question but a statement, and Mary felt that he was hinting at more than he was actually saying, and she felt the blood rush to her cheeks as her temper rose. 'Somehow, I've an idea he won't be disappointed,' she replied bitingly. He could make what he wanted of that! she told herself furiously.

Rafael's lips thinned for a second, then he gave her an unpleasant smile. 'Yes, you've certainly made your mark there, but don't be too sure of yourself. You are in my father's house, but it is me you will eventually have to deal with. It might pay you to remember that,' he bit out.

Mary went white and felt as if he had dealt her a swift blow across the face. The gloves were off now and there was no mistaking the fact that he was handing out a warning to her to watch her step. His father might have been taken in by her, but he knew better, and whatever she had hoped to bring off in the financial stakes depended entirely upon his goodwill, not his father's.

He did not have to put it in so many words; it was there in the way that he was looking at her—had been, ever since he had overheard Derek's outburst. Mary knew that he did not have a good opinion of her, but his scathing condemnation of her was entirely unjustified and she wished with all her heart that she could show him that she was not interested in any financial

gain by taking Paul home with her on the very next
flight, and telling this arrogant man that it was he who
ought to watch his step if he wished to communicate
with his nephew—let alone see him! She swallowed
convulsively. She could do none of these things, not
now, and he knew it, only he would put an entirely
different interpretation on why she had to put up with
this miserable situation, she thought bleakly.

Her white face and bleak expression was not lost on
Rafael, who took it as a sign of capitulation on her
part. 'You will please wear one of the dresses provided,'
he said curtly, and added grandly, 'the choice is up to
you.'

It took a second or so for Mary to recover from this
dictatorial statement, or rather order, for that was what
it was. His hand was on the door handle when she managed to gasp out in a voice that showed her outraged
dignity, 'As you say, the choice is up to me.' Her furious
eyes swept back to the dresses on the bed, resting
scathingly on the fine lace of one of them, and then
on one of a gossamer material—all very expensive.
'Even if I hadn't anything to wear, I wouldn't wear
those!' She glared back at Rafael now standing stiffly
by the door. 'You ought to have ascertained my likes
and dislikes, Señor Alvarados,' she flung at him, 'and
not one of those is suitable!'

She turned away from him abruptly, willing him to
go and leave her in peace before she burst into tears of
utter frustration. If she broke down in front of him she
would never forgive herself. Don Emilio, she thought
bitterly, would never have been part of this. He would
have had the sensitivity to realise how much the gesture
would have hurt her. She couldn't afford to buy clothes
like that—never would be able to afford them. If her

off-the-peg clothes offended his guests, he would be more likely to side with her than with them, instinctively she knew this, but Rafael Alvarados was not Don Emilio. She felt suddenly sick of the whole stupid confrontation. 'Thank you, anyway, for the thought,' she said in a low voice that echoed her bitterness, and added on a firmer note, 'Don't worry, I shall not disgrace you.'

'As you wish!' answered Rafael in a savage voice. The next moment she heard the door close with a force that showed his fury at not getting his own way, and must have cost him a lot of self-control to avoid slamming it.

For several minutes after he had gone Mary stood looking at the dresses and felt a distinct urge to fling them out of the window one after the other, but managed to control this primitive urge to get her own back on the autocratic Rafael Alvarados. She swept them off the bed with one contemptous gesture and threw them on to a chair. Tomorrow she would ask the woman called Maria to return them from wherever they had come from—or better still, she thought maliciously, ask her to give them to Rafael Alvarados!

She sank slowly on to the bed; she would do neither, so what was the point of pretending that she would? Her eye caught the rose print dress that she had chosen to wear that evening, and went back to the three beautiful gowns now lying in disarray on the chair. Tears of utter frustration filled her eyes. There was simply no comparison. Against those elegant models her dress looked like some kind of beach wear.

She shook her head to dispel the tears and got up from the bed and walked with a determined step towards the dresses. One was a soft blue with fine lace at the neck and at the cuffs. The next one she examined had a square neckline and close-fitting top with a swirl-ing skirt of a sort of gossamer material. The colour was a pale yellow, and although it would have suited her colouring, Mary somehow did not feel it was right for her. The third dress was of velvet and the colour of deep burgundy. It was absolutely plain with long sleeves that widened at the wrists. The neck was a simple vee, but modestly so.

If she wore any of the dresses it would be the velvet one, of that she was sure. A glance at the label inside with the name of the salon printed in embossed gold not only told her that the gowns were original models, but were her size.

She was in agony of indecision; how could she pos-sibly wear the rose print when confronted by this show of splendour? Her hands folded into fists and her nails bit into the soft skin of her palm. She hated Rafael Alvarados for his insensitivity in making her feel shoddy. She would have been quite happy to wear the dress she had chosen had she not seen this finery.

But how would she have felt in the company of other well-dressed women? Her teeth caught her soft bottom lip; uncomfortable, that was what she would have felt! She might not be rich, but she had as much pride as any other woman. She thought of her sister Sheila and how she would have felt in the same position. A slow sigh escaped her as she acknowledged the fact that as Paul's mother she would have had no hesitation in accepting the gift, and would have accepted with far more grace than Mary had. In all probability she would have been delighted and not looked for ulterior motives behind the gift.

Mary ran a tentative finger along the rich velvet material, then holding it up against her, she walked over to the long mirror and studied the effect. There was no denying that the colour suited her, and she drew in a deep breath. She would wear the dress—not for Rafael Alvarados—but for Don Emilio's sake. Just this once, she told herself, she would let the haughty Rafael ride roughshod over her pride. What did she care what he thought anyway? He would have to return to his business affairs sooner or later, and all she had to do was to hold on to her temper. Although, she thought sadly, she hadn't come out too well from their last confrontation. She squared her shoulders. From now on she would keep her distance from the infuriating man, and no matter what it cost her, treat him with cool politeness.

When the gong sounded a little later, she gave herself a last look in the mirror before going down to dinner. Her hair was now pinned back in the french pleat style that she used for school and looked prim and neat. The dress gave her an added dignity, fitting her slim figure like a glove. It also helped to give her the necessary courage to face up to Rafael's satirical look that he was bound to favour her with on sight of the dress.

The lounge was empty when Mary arrived, but she could hear voices coming from the patio from which she identified Don Emilio's soft Spanish intonations and then Rafael's deep answering tone that sounded lazy and a little amused. A feminine chuckle told Mary that the guests had arrived and that at least one of them was feminine.

She did not venture out to join them but stayed in the lounge, for going by the fact that a tray of drinks had been laid out, she presumed they would shortly be gathering there for the customary drink before dinner.

She filled in the waiting period by examining a small piece of exquisite pottery that she thought might be Dresden, and was just about to ascertain this by looking at the markings at its base when they arrived.

'Ah, Mary!' exclaimed Don Emilio. 'I hope we have not kept you waiting long?' he queried, and gave what she could only interpret as an appreciative look at her. He was pleased by her appearance and somehow managed to convey this to her without verbal comment, and Mary felt uplifted and glad that she had not let her pride prevent her from wearing the dress.

The girl who stood beside him favoured Mary with a critical examination, her dark and very lovely eyes did not echo the smile on her full red lips, and this Mary duly noted. Behind her and still deep in conversation with Rafael was an elderly man who could have been the girl's father, for there was a certain likeness between them.

Whatever subject the men were discussing was broken off at a slight gesture from Don Emilio, who then carried out the introductions.

It was not until Mary held her hand out to shake the slim white hand of Señorita Isabel Juana Ruiz that she realised that she was still holding the small piece of pottery and she had to hastily replace it before accepting the proffered hand. She felt embarrassed enough without glancing up to find Rafael's fastidious eyes upon her, and a slight flush mounted her cheeks. He had to notice that, hadn't he? she thought miserably.

The Ruiz family, Mary discovered, were old friends of the Alvarados family, and made her feel even more of an alien than before, although Don Emilio did his best to make certain that the conversation took place in

English and that Mary was able to follow and enter into whatever subject was introduced. He was not entirely successful in this, however, as Isabel would every now and again burst into her native tongue when speaking to Rafael in spite of a frowning Don Emilio.

It was not because she did not have a good command of English. She was perfectly articulate in the language, and Mary could only assume that she was determined not to be subdued by Mary's presence.

For Mary it was an uncomfortable meal, and she was glad when it was time to retire to the *salón* for coffee afterwards. Her discomfiture was increased when she saw Rafael pick up the piece of pottery she had handled earlier and move it from the position she had left it, to what she noticed with no little chagrin was its original position on a small antique table.

It had been done in an almost absentminded way, yet Mary was sure that here again he was underlying her inferior position in his father's house. She could look but not touch, seemed to be the message her highly sensitive feelings deduced from this action. Never again would she give him cause to pass such a message on to her, she vowed, and wondered satirically if it were permissible for her to sit down in such exalted company!

When the story of the discovery of Enrique's son and the subsequent events that had culminated in Paul and Mary's arrival the previous day was exhausted, the conversation turned to other matters. Mary for one was distinctly relieved to have the subject dropped, and she was sure that she was not the only one who felt that way. Isabel had been very reticent on the subject, and going by her earlier animated contributions to the conversation directed mainly at Rafael, this lapse was noticeable, at least by Mary, but not apparently by Don Emilio, to whom the discovery was nothing short of a miracle.

Now that the subject was changed Isabel reverted to her earlier sparkling form. Mary, sitting quietly on her own in an armchair opposite the lounger where Isabel and Rafael sat, was able to study them at her leisure, particularly as Don Emilio, who had elected to sit on a high-backed chair next to his friend Señor Ruiz, was now deep in conversation with him on the merits of a new vintage recently introduced into the Alvarados range.

As far as Isabel and Rafael were concerned she might not have been present, she thought with a wry inward smile. No sooner was the thought there than Rafael suddenly turned towards her and asked her if she swam. Mary was disconcerted for a second or so as the question had taken her unawares, but she answered politely enough, aware that Don Emilio had heard the question and was waiting for her answer too. She replied that she did, but she was not a strong swimmer.

Isabel had shrugged at this. 'I am not Olympic material either,' she said, giving Rafael a sideways grin for his benefit only. 'But I do manage to enjoy myself.'

'Good,' replied Rafael in clipped tones. 'We were thinking of having a bathing party this weekend. Enrique tells me he can be relied upon not to sink,' he added with a twist of amusement on his lips.

'That just about sums up his accomplishments in that line,' replied Mary with a smile. 'He needs a lot more practice before I would let him in on his own.'

Whether or not it was her protective attitude towards Paul that suddenly turned what had been a conciliatory attempt on Rafael's part back to hostility, Mary did not know. She did know that the mention of Paul had brought back Isabel's reticence, and was pleased when she adroitly changed the conversation and spoke in a low voice to Rafael in Spanish.

By now Don Emilio had resumed his discussion with Señor Ruiz, and Mary realised with a spurt of anger that that had been the only reason Rafael had directed that question at her. His father must have somehow wordlessly reminded him of his manners, and once he had made sure that Mary was being included in their conversation, he had been able to indulge in a long talk with his friend.

If it were not for hurting Don Emilio, Mary would have got up and walked right out of that room. She did not attempt to listen to whatever Isabel was saying to Rafael. If she had done there was a distinct possibility that she would have understood much of their conversation, but she was no eavesdropper. The very fact that Isabel had declined to use English proved that her words were for Rafael alone. It would not occur to her, thought Mary, that the plain English woman was as conversant in her tongue as Isabel was in English.

As she watched Rafael answer something Isabel had said, she saw how his normally stern features were now relaxed, and it was with something of a start that she acknowledged that he was flirting mildly with the girl. She frowned on this thought; perhaps flirting was not the right word—teasing, perhaps? but anyway, enjoying himself.

Her attention then focused on Isabel, engaged at that moment in gazing up into Rafael's amused eyes, her red lips pouting at something he had said. There was no doubt that she was lovely, thought Mary, and could obviously afford to dress in a way that enhanced her looks. Her dress was of a soft shade of pink, the material being some kind of silk that shone with every movement and fitted her slim body to perfection. Mary wondered how old she was; a little older than she had thought at first sight, she mused, and that meant that she must be in her early twenties, say twenty-two or three.

Old enough, thought Mary, to be married and with a family, for Spanish girls married young, particularly the wealthy ones, care being taken to provide them with a husband equally suitably endowed. But Isabel was not married, and there couldn't have been a shortage of applicants for her hand, not with those looks.

Her gaze turned to Rafael; was he the reason she was still a *señorita*? He had said something about disappointing his father. Was it because he had failed to pop the question? The families were old friends; in all probability they had grown up together. Marrying someone you grew up with very rarely brought happiness, surmised Mary. Only on extremely rare occasions; you knew too much about each other for a start, she thought with an inward smile.

'Can I get you a liqueur, my dear?' asked Don Emilio gently, directing a furious look towards Rafael. 'I can recommend Tia Maria,' he added with a smile at her.

'No, thank you,' replied Mary. 'I still have the delicious taste of your coffee with me, anything else would spoil it,' she smiled.

'Then I shall have some more coffee made for you,' exclaimed Don Emilio gallantly.

'Thank you, but I've had ample,' replied Mary. 'As a matter of fact I was just wondering whether I might be excused. I'm not really used to late hours, you know,' she tacked on hastily on seeing the look of consternation on Don Emilio's face and guessing the reason behind it.

Put like that there was not much he could do about it, but Mary could see that he was not entirely convinced that her reason to retire was not just an excuse to save herself from further embarrassment.

His kindly eyes searched the candid grey ones, but there was nothing in Mary's expression to suggest any ulterior motive behind her wish to retire. He gave her an indulgent smile. 'Very well,' he replied with a regretful note in his voice. 'For this one occasion, you may be excused. If I were younger and of a better constitution, I would suggest we take a walk in the garden before you retire,' his elegant hands spread out in an eloquent gesture. 'As it is, I must conserve my strength for future occasions.'

Grateful for her release from what was becoming an intolerable situation, Mary gave him a twinkling smile. 'Some other time, perhaps?' she murmured, and was rewarded by an answering smile from Don Emilio. Mary then made her escape, and was a little surprised at the way Rafael stood up as she took her leave, showing that he had some gentlemanly virtues left, even if it was only instinctive!

The calm she had forced upon herself in order to forestall Don Emilio's suspicions now evaporated, and she felt curiously flat and numb inside as she made her way back to her room.

When she had closed the door behind her she gave a sigh of thankfulness that her ordeal was over, for it had been an ordeal. As for the bathing party that Rafael had mentioned, if he thought he was giving her a treat—or that she ought to appreciate such consideration on his part—then he was off the mark. Far from

looking forward to it, she dreaded it. And as for that
sulky little *señorita*—Mary's hands clenched into fists.
Anyone would think she was a rival for Rafael's affections, the way she had treated Mary that evening. Oh,
she had been very subtle about it, condescending too,
and that was worse.

She might just as well have worn the rose print dress,
Mary thought furiously, since her treatment could not
have been much worse than what she would have suffered if she had worn it. At least, she thought angrily,
it might have provided a reason for such downright condescending behaviour on the part of Rafael and Isabel.

When she recalled the way Isabel had continually
lapsed into her native tongue in spite of Don Emilio's
obvious wish that they should converse in English,
Mary felt even angrier; Rafael could have done something about that, she acknowledged silently, but he also
had no wish to pander to his father's code of behaviour,
and had allowed Isabel to indulge in what could only
be termed as an outright snub to Mary's presence.

Mary wished she had had the presence of mind to
wish them goodnight in Spanish. Their reaction would
have repaid all the discomfort she had endured that
evening. She spent a few moments savouring this
thought, then shook her head wearily. The fact that
she had taken the trouble to learn Spanish would only
give Rafael Alvarados another stick to beat her with.
In his eyes there could be only one reason as to why
she had applied herself to this task. He would reason
that although her family had lost contact with his
brother, they must have known that he came of a
wealthy family, and had nursed hopes of Enrique
eventually seeking them out, or alternatively, present-

ing the child to him when they had traced his where-
abouts.

The true fact of the matter was that Mary and Sheila
had been planning to take a holiday in Spain, having
saved for months for what would have been, for them,
a holiday of a lifetime. Fate, however, had intervened,
and Sheila had met Enrique, and Mary had never had a
chance to put her knowledge of Spanish to the test—
not until now—but here again it appeared fate was
having a say in the matter, and she was being forced to
abide by the invisible yet entirely binding set of circumstances dealt out to her.

Mary drew a hand across her forehead. It was very
close in the room, and she was about to go across to the
window and let in the night air when she remembered
Don Emilio's remarks about a walk in the garden. Her
lips twisted into an ironical smile on the thought that
perhaps he was giving Rafael a prompting, hoping that
he would offer to stand in for his father, and if so, he
ought to have known better!

There was nothing to stop her acting on Don Emilio's
sugestion with or without an escort, and she decided
that a walk in the cool of the evening would certainly
help to dispel her depression. She certainly wasn't
going to help matters by sitting in her room dwelling
on them.

With a light cardigan over her shoulders she made
her way down to the back of the villa and let herself
out of the side door she had discovered during her
wanderings earlier that day, and followed the same
route back to the fountain.

It was as well that she had a good memory, as the
night was a moonless one, yet the brilliant stars above
her gave her just enough light to make out the garden

paths, and she was quite pleased with herself when she came upon the fountain now lit with a soft blue light that enhanced its setting. Had she not found the fountain that morning it was doubtful whether she would have come across it at night, as the tall trees that screened it effectively hid what might have been a guiding light to its destination.

A sense of peace enfolded her as she sat watching the dancing droplets of the now pale blue water as it showered down from its propelled height. The fragrant perfume of numerous flowers drifted around her and she felt that she was in a place of enchantment.

There was nothing but joy and hope for the future in such a place as this. Misunderstandings and pride had no hold here. The fountain was man-made, but the night was eternal, and as lovely as the fountain was, without nature's backcloth, it was nothing. The same, Mary thought, could be said of her troubles. They would only exist if she allowed them to, if she let her pride take precedence over all else. As long as Paul— here, she mentally corrected herself, Enrique, was happy, and of that there could be no doubt, why should she concern herself with anything else?

She had no awareness of the passage of time, until she dimly heard the slamming of car doors some distance away, and although she was loth to move from her enchanted surroundings, she knew that it must be quite late and time for her to go.

With a reluctant sigh she got up and started on the return journey back to the villa. She would come here each night, she told herself, and whatever pinpricks the day had held for her, she was sure they would all be eased away in the midst of that silent magical atmosphere. She might have been being fanciful, but she had felt very close to Sheila there. As if she was pleased that Mary had brought Enrique back to where he belonged, and no doubt his father would have felt the same way about things, she mused as she neared the villa.

The sound of voices stopped her in her tracks as she was about to cross a short stretch of lawn between her and the villa. She stood still for a moment or so to ascertain where the voices were coming from, and realised with dismay that Don Emilio and Rafael were on the patio, probably enjoying a last cigar before going to bed.

This in itself was not what was troubling Mary, but she would have to pass the lighted area of the patio before she could reach the villa. This fact was borne in upon her as soon as she had rounded the bend of thick shrubbery that separated the garden from the villa precincts.

With an exasperated sigh she looked for some cover she could use to enable her to approach the villa unobserved, but there was none. She would simply have to wait until they had gone back into the villa again.

The smell of cigar smoke drifted towards her and was not unpleasant; she hoped they had not just lit their cigars but were on the point of finishing them. She frowned on the thought that Don Emilio ought not to be up so late, and then wondered whether it was quite so late as she thought it was. Even if she had been wearing her watch she would not have been able to make out where the hands were pointing, since the lighted area just in front of her made her surroundings darker than they might otherwise have been.

'Are you going to marry her?' The question came loud and clear towards the startled Mary, who froze on the spot when she realised that the men must have been standing near the french windows opening on to the lawn and had now moved on to the patio.

The question had been asked by Don Emilio, and in dismay Mary distinctly heard Rafael's abrupt, 'No, I have not changed my mind, Padre, and am not likely to.'

For the first time since Mary had learnt the Spanish language she miserably wished she had not been such a brilliant student. At least she could have remained in ignorance of their conversation. For one tense second she debated whether to make her presence known to them. She could slip silently back to the garden and come back and openly cross the lawn towards them. She could say something about taking up Don Emilio's suggestion of a walk in the garden—that was the absolute truth—but would not, she thought bitterly, be believed by the sceptical Rafael. He would be bound to wonder just how much of their conversation she had overheard.

She bit her lower lip in an agony of indecision; if she was going to do that she ought to do it now before anything else was said, as both men had fallen silent. But she did not move; the thought of Rafael's all too discerning eyes held her utterly immobile. She was hopeless at brazening anything out, she would be unable to meet either his or Don Emilio's eyes, and would probably say something stupid that would completely give her away.

'I am not sorry,' Don Emilio replied, after apparently giving the matter some thought. 'She is too young for you—would always be. She's a pretty woman, but when you've said that, you've said everything.'

Mary was sure that it was Isabel that they were discussing, and she fervently hoped that that would be the end of such a personal discussion, and if not, that they would move back into the villa before continuing.

Neither of these hopes were realised as she heard Don Emilio go on to say, 'Then you must be quite firm about it. Do not encourage her. I realise it is not easy, but you must make the situation quite clear to her.'

'I fail to see what I can do, apart from what I have already done,' replied Rafael, sounding bored with the subject. 'She still clings to the outdated notion that I should honour the arrangement she had with Enrique.'

Mary's breath caught in a gasp; arrangement with Enrique? Her breath came out slowly as she caught the implication behind Rafael's words. Isabel was the girl Enrique had been engaged to! Little wonder she had not welcomed Mary with open arms! And Enrique's son? Mary wondered; what would be her reaction to Paul? The likeness alone was surely a reason to make her resentful of the pair of them, even though Mary was not his mother.

She closed her eyes. Surely it was time they finished their cigars and went to bed. Not for the world would she now reveal her presence. She was even afraid to move in case she accidentally stepped on a dry twig and gave her presence away. Her embarrassment would be total if she were discovered.

By now she was beginning to feel a little chilly, and knew that her legs would soon start to complain at the stiff upright position she was trying to maintain in order to keep absolutely still. Don Emilio's next statement, however, took all thought of discomfort away and left her numb with shock.

'It's not Isabel I wanted to discuss with you,' said Don Emilio, just as Mary thought they were about to go into the villa, for she distinctly heard the creak of one of the cane chairs and had presumed Don Emilio had stood up. In fact it must have been the opposite and he must have sat down—either that, or Rafael had decided to take the weight off his feet and join his father. 'Although,' continued Don Emilio thoughtfully, 'I did need to know your intentions in that direction.' There was a long pause after this, and then he added, 'I want you to seriously consider offering marriage to Mary Allis.'

If you were in their place what would you do?

Jeanette...

Though she has survived a heart-wrenching tragedy, is there more unhappiness in store for Jeanette? She is hopelessly in love with a man who is inaccessible to her. Her story will come alive in the pages of "Beyond the Sweet Waters" by Anne Hampson.

Juliet...

Rather than let her father choose her husband, she ran...ran into the life of the haughty duke and his intriguing household on a Caribbean island. It's an intimate story that will stir you as you read "The Arrogant Duke" by Anne Mather.

Laurel...

There was no turning back for Laurel. She was playing out a charade with the arrogant plantation owner, and the stakes were "love". It's all part of a thrilling romantic adventure called "Teachers Must Learn" by Nerina Hilliard.

Fern...

She tried to escape to a new life...a new world...now she was faced with a loveless marriage of convenience. How long could she wait for the love she so strongly craved to come to her... Live with Fern... love with Fern...in the exciting "Cap Flamingo" by Violet Winspear.

Jeanette, Juliet, Laurel, Fern...these are some of the memorable people who come alive in the pages of Harlequin Romance novels. And now, without leaving your home, you can share their most intimate moments!

It's the easiest and most convenient way to get every one of the exciting Harlequin Romance novels! And now with a home subscription plan you won't miss any of these true-to-life stories, and you don't even have to go out looking for them.

Get your
Harlequin Romance
Home Subscription NOW!

- Never miss a title!
- Get them first—straight from the presses!
- No additional costs for home delivery!
- These first 4 novels are yours FREE!

Postes Canada

021

Canada Post

Harlequin Reader Service
Stratford (Ontario)
N5A 6W2

Business Reply Mail

No Postage Stamp Necessary if Mailed in Canada

Postage will be paid by

CHAPTER SIX

It was a wonder that Mary's legs continued to support her, and she vaguely wondered why she did not just sink to the ground in a dead faint as her Victorian counterparts were said to have done with surprising ease, for far less reason.

There was no such merciful release for her, and she took the silence that followed this mind-boggling suggestion as distinct proof that she was not the only one suffering from shock!

When Rafael did answer it was obvious by his carefully phrased words that he was of the opinion that his father had taken leave of his senses. 'I would prefer to ignore such a ridiculous suggestion,' he said curtly. 'It is not necessary. You have the boy, and even,' he added furiously, 'if there were a good reason for such an alliance, I can assure you, Father, that I would seek other methods of keeping Enrique here where he belongs.'

'I do not understand your vehemence,' said Don Emilio with a weary note in his voice. 'Or what you can possibly hold against Mary. I find her to be a quiet, well brought up young woman. You can do worse, my son. Oh, I'm not suggesting a passionate alliance. That perhaps may come in time, but Enrique must bear the Alvarados name. It is imperative!' This was said with as much vehemence as Rafael had used in reply to his father.

'If that is all that is worrying you, then arrangements

97

can be made to have his name changed by deed poll. No other method is required; all that is needed is the agreement of both parties, in this case you or myself, and Mary Allis,' replied Rafael calmly.

'What if she marries?' demanded Don Emilio. 'And what if they decide to keep Enrique with them? What then?' he asked irritably.

'Considering the lady is already bespoken—a fact I must confess I had previously overlooked,' Rafael answered with a trace of relief in his voice, 'I do not think you will receive any opposition from that quarter. I rather think that we will find that Miss Allis's fiancé will be more than willing to relinquish all rights over the child's future.'

'Mary is engaged?' queried Don Emilio, the surprise in his voice quite evident. 'But she distinctly told me there was no one. You must be mistaken, Rafael. I am certain that she would not lie to me.'

'And I am certain,' replied Rafael in a hard voice, 'that she would, providing it suited her purpose. You have too trusting a nature, my father,' he added on a softer note. 'It is as well that I am here. Come now, forget all this nonsense. All will be well, I promise you. Now come inside into the warm, the air is getting chilly now.'

The light was suddenly dowsed and Mary found herself trembling with shock bordering on rage. Her hands clenched into fists by her side. Of all the hateful interfering, autocratic males, Rafael Alvarados was top of the list!

It was not in her nature to eavesdrop, but since she had had no choice but to overhear such a conversation, and the fact that it concerned herself, it made her grateful that she had been afforded such an opportunity.

She didn't care about Rafael Alvarados, but she did care about Don Emilio: What would he think of her now? And for goodness' sake, how could she put the matter right and explain that she had broken off her engagement to Derek before coming to Spain?

A few moments' thought, however, told her that she could do nothing about it whatsoever. She could hardly bring the subject up of her own volition, and how she could bring herself to act normally in the presence of that obnoxious man Rafael Alvarados, let alone speak to him, was beyond her comprehension. Yet she had to, somehow she had to force herself to be polite to him when she would dearly have loved to slap that arrogant face. Offer her marriage indeed! As if she would accept! It was just as well that he felt as abhorred as she did at the very thought. Her lovely grey eyes sparkled with temper. It was a great pity that she was not going to be given the opportunity of turning him down, for that at least would give her some consolation for her treatment at his hands.

After giving what she hoped was a reasonable lapse of time after the men had left the patio, Mary slipped into the villa and went to her room. As tired as she was, it was a long time before she fell asleep.

When she awoke the following morning, the sound of water splashing coming from the bathroom told her that Enrique was once again in the capable hands of Maria. He must have slept late that morning as he had not called in on her as he usually did. Mary's lips twisted in an ironical smile on the thought that perhaps he was growing up. There was no doubt that since his arrival at the villa he had grown in confidence. He had never complained to Mary about the lack of a father, but had accepted what she had told him about there now being just the two of them. At home, that was, but there must have been times when he had felt the loss keenly. It could not have been easy for him at school; children could be cruel and had an uncanny knack of hitting out where it hurt most.

She recalled small incidents in the past, and how he would arrive home dishevelled with bruised cheeks, and once a black eye, shortly after he had attended school. Mary had tried to convince herself that this sort of thing was normal—boys did fight, didn't they? In spite of his small stature he had a temper to match the tallest of his opponents and enough pride to give a good account of himself in a skirmish. He would never tell her the cause of the fights, but would mutter darkly that old so-and-so would think twice before starting a fight with him again.

Things had gradually settled down, there were no more fights, and thinking about it now, Mary realised that he had fought his way through to acceptance of a kind, but his pride made him hold back from any closer relationship with his contemporaries. All, that was, except Michael who lived a few doors away. Michael's father was in the Navy, a career that necessitated long periods away from home, and Mary had wondered if it was this circumstance that had formed the basis of their friendship. Whatever the reason was, she was extremely grateful for the friendship.

'Have you brought my swimming things?' demanded Enrique, rushing into her bedroom and breaking off her musings. 'Juan wants to swim this morning.'

Mary cast her mind back to the time when she had packed their clothes and had to shake her head. She had been in too much of a rush to consider such things as swimming costumes. 'We'll have to buy you one,' she said hopefully, and looked at Maria standing behind him and waiting to take him down to breakfast.

Maria answered the unspoken question Mary had asked her by nodding her head vigorously and fixing her black eyes on Enrique. 'I fix you, you see—come along, *niño*,' and gave the relieved Mary a smile as the child gave a whoop of joy that transformed his earlier bleak expression, and took him off to breakfast.

If the *niño* was happy, so too was Maria, Mary mused as she recalled the look of tenderness in her dark eyes as she had looked at Enrique's son. She now knew that her earlier assumption that Maria had looked after Rafael and Enrique when they were children was correct, for Paul had told her so.

By the time Mary was up and dressed, Enrique was off to meet Juan, who had promised to meet him shortly after nine by the vineyards that separated Juan's home from the villa. For the first time since she had taken on Enrique's upbringing, Mary found herself absolutely free to follow her own inclinations, and she wasn't sure that she liked it.

Like it or not, she would just have to get used to it, she told herself as she made her way down to the patio for breakfast. As long as she was there when he needed her, then that was all that was required. Although, she thought sadly, she did feel a little hurt at the way he had formed such an immediate attachment to his uncle, and although he stood a little in awe of his grandfather there was no denying that he respected him, and that on closer acquaintance would become very fond of him. Then there was Maria, the old servant who had taken over Mary's duties so smoothly that it was barely noticeable, except of course to Mary, who had felt a little piqued at the way Enrique had accepted the ministrations of a stranger without a murmur.

She was just telling herself that she ought to be grateful that he was happy and his future was now assured, when she saw that Don Emilio was waiting on the patio to take breakfast with her. The sight of that upright figure drove all other thoughts from her mind and recalled vividly the conversation she had overheard the previous evening.

It was all Mary could do to push the memory away from her as she took his hand and enquired after his health that morning, adding quickly that she hoped his early appearance was a sign of improvement. The words were almost babbled in her anxiety to present a normal greeting to him, and realising this, she looked away from him and sat down at the table.

At first the conversation centred on Enrique and how he was settling down, and Mary was able to answer quite truthfully that there was no problem there.

'And you, Mary?' he asked, his dark eyes searching the candid grey ones.

This question was not so easy to answer, and Mary was well aware of the reasoning behind this seemingly innocent question. 'It's different for me,' she began slowly, accepting a cup of coffee from him. 'I mean, it doesn't really matter about me, does it? I'm quite content for the moment to accept your kind hospitality, but later,' she hesitated, 'when Enrique has settled in, I see no reason why I should not return home.' Her fingers gripped her cup tightly at the mere thought of returning without him, yet it had to be; he belonged there, and she did not, it was as simple as that. Even without the despicable Rafael's company, she simply could not envisage herself settling down to a sort of dowager's existence relying on hand-outs from the

Alvarados family. She almost shuddered at the thought.

Don Emilio frowned after this brief but telling statement of hers. 'You are family, Mary,' he said quietly. 'Please do not speak of hospitality. This is your home as much as it is Enrique's, and I wish you to regard it as such.'

Mary felt a lump gathering in her throat. Any minute now she would burst into tears, for there was no doubting the sincerity behind his words. She laid an impulsive hand over the slim white one of Don Emilio. 'I didn't mean to make it sound like that,' she said quickly, and shook her head, impatient at her inability to express herself in a more understanding way. 'I very much appreciate the way you have welcomed us here. Oh dear,' she exclaimed sadly, as she saw that Don Emilio's expression remained a frowning one. 'That doesn't sound right either, does it? Please don't look so cross. What I'm trying to say is, don't worry about me,' she gave him a tremulous smile. 'I'm old enough to look after myself, you know, and I haven't done too badly up to now. Paul——' she held out her hands in a helpless gesture. 'I can't seem to get into the habit of calling him by his first name yet, but no doubt it will come in time.' She took a deep breath. 'Enrique will stay, that I can promise you. I do believe,' she added, trying to inject a note of jocularity into her voice, 'that I could leave tomorrow and he wouldn't miss me!' She shrugged. 'So much for thinking one is indispensable!'

She could almost feel the relief Don Emilio felt at her assurance that his grandchild would not be torn from him, now or at any time in the future. As for her half amused statement that Enrique would not miss her if she left, this he did not agree with and said so. 'Until he is sick,' he said gently. 'Or something happens that he does not understand.' He gave an expressive shrug. 'Now he is fully occupied. Everything is new, and he is in a world of discovery.' He smiled at her. 'I shall not say that I hope the experience wears off in time. I want him to be happy here, but he regards you as his mother, Mary, and there can be no substitute for that,' he reminded her quietly.

They were both silent for a few minutes after this, and Don Emilio, buttering a crisp roll, suddenly looked up at her engaged upon the same task. 'Are you certain that you couldn't settle down here, Mary? It's early days yet, you know. Give it time. It's not as if you had a particular reason for leaving, is it?' he asked.

Mary's hand holding the butter knife stilled at the question. He was giving her a chance to verify or dispute Rafael's assertion that she was engaged, but she had to be careful here and not rush her fences and let him know that she was perfectly aware of the reasoning behind his seemingly innocent question. On the other hand she couldn't afford to miss the opportunity to put the record straight, and she might never get another chance like this. 'Not now,' she said slowly, deciding that honesty was her best policy. 'I was engaged, you know.' She looked down at the knife still in her hand and laid it back on the butter dish. 'It didn't work out,' she added quietly. There wasn't much she could add to that, as it was the truth.

Don Emilio's dark eyes studied her frank grey eyes. 'Why didn't it work out, Mary?' he asked gently. 'Was it because of the child?'

Mary's start did not go unobserved by her attentive companion, who nodded his head slowly as if satisfied on this point at least. 'Now that Enrique's future is assured, are you hoping for a reconciliation?' he asked softly.

'No!' answered Mary unhesitatingly with a certain amount of determination in her voice. 'There's no possibility of that happening whatsoever.' She smiled at Don Emilio brightly, wanting to dispel her earlier vehemence that might just have looked as if he had touched upon a raw spot in her heart. In fact it was just the reverse. 'Thinking back,' she went on musingly, 'I don't honestly know why we ever got engaged in the first place.' She frowned. 'I think we both wanted security. Well, I did, anyway,' she added honestly. 'But it soon became obvious that it wasn't going to work out and the only thing to do was to end it.'

The way Don Emilio continued to give her what she could only interpret as a sympathetic look told her that he was not entirely convinced that her heart had remained unscathed at the break-up of her romance, and his next words proved this. 'Poor Mary,' he said softly. 'It hasn't been too easy for you, has it?' He caught hold of her hand and gave it a gentle squeeze. 'That is all in the past now. You must look forward and not back. But one thing I would ask of you, and that is, do not make any hasty decisions about leaving. It is time someone else took over the reins, and that is what I intend to do. From now on, I want you to enjoy yourself. You must explore Seville. We have many wonderful works of art preserved through the centuries and we are proud of our heritage.' He smiled at her. 'You would not want to forgo such an experience, surely?'

Mary felt as if there was a tight band around her throat, but she managed to smile back at him before answering huskily, 'Of course not! I'm looking forward to seeing Seville. I particularly want to see your beautiful cathedral. It's the oldest Gothic building in Europe, isn't it?' she asked.

It appeared that she had chosen the right subject to turn Don Emilio's thoughts in other directions and it helped her over the thin ice she felt she had been skating over earlier. As she listened to her host's enthusiastic narrative on the history of the Cathedral, Mary's thoughts slightly wandered from the subject and she wondered if she had been wise to refute his suggestion that she had been hoping for a reconciliation with Derek. Wouldn't it have been better if she had let him think that she had hopes in that direction? It would certainly put an end to his hoped-for alliance between Rafael and herself if it did nothing else. However, on second thoughts, she decided that it was better that she had told the truth. She had done with falsehood. Had Don Emilio's schemes involved anyone else but Rafael Alvarados, Mary might have had cause to worry; as it was, she had nothing to fear and could safely rely on him to firmly scotch any such ill-conceived plot.

When breakfast was over Don Emilio took his leave of her, mentioning that it was the morning the doctor called, and solicitously enquired how she intended to fill her morning, to which Mary answered with a twinkle in her eye that she thought she might wander down to the swimming pool to keep an eye on his grandchild.

Her words produced a smile of appreciation from Don Emilio, and as he took his leave of her Mary noticed that his figure was just a little more erect than before, and his step just that little lighter. There was an assurance about his bearing that said more than words could ever say, and she felt a spurt of pure pleasure at the thought that she had contributed a small amount towards his recovery.

Her step was lighter too as she went in search of Enrique and as the sound of children's laughter drifted towards her as she approached the pool her mouth relaxed in a smile, for children's laughter was infectious.

When she saw a lounger placed by the side of the pool, she saw that she had not been the only one who had had the thought of keeping an eye on the boys.

A plump blonde woman rose to greet her as she neared the pool area and held out her hand with a welcoming smile on her face. 'I'm Juan's mother,' she said with a slight lilt in her voice that spoke of the Welsh hills. 'And I presume that you are Miss Allis?'

Mary took the proffered hand and smiled back at the woman. 'Please call me Mary,' she said, feeling a surge of happiness at meeting a countrywoman of hers, and knowing instinctively that they were going to like each other.

'Thank you, I'm Joan,' replied Señora Santos in a tone of voice that echoed Mary's sentiments. 'How are you coping with the heat?' she asked solicitously as she pulled another lounger up next to hers for Mary's use. 'I must confess it took me a long time to get used to it when I first came here. Now I'm used to it, but I still have to remember to wear a hat when I go out.' She looked at Mary's empty hands and then at her bare head. 'Never go anywhere without a hat, Mary,' she scolded her gently. 'Not between July and September, anyway.'

Mary gave a rueful smile. 'I shall have to tie one round my neck,' she said. 'It would be stupid of me to learn the hard way with sunstroke, wouldn't it?'

At that moment Juan rushed up and surveyed Mary with dark shy eyes. He was a plump, dark version of his mother, but his hair was already showing signs of turn-

ing a lighter colour and would probably be of a chestnut hue when he was older.

'This is Enrique's mother,' said Joan, giving Mary
a conspiratorial look that told Mary that she was aware
of the true relationship between them. 'Say "how do
you do," Juan.'

Juan's small plump hand was held out tentatively
as he gravely repeated the salutation, and Mary was
tempted to reply in his native tongue but resisted the
temptation and replied, 'I am very pleased to meet you,
Juan,' with the same amount of gravity slightly under-
lined by a twinkle in her eyes.

'Juan can swim the whole length of the pool!' exclaimed Enrique, rushing up to join them, his slight
wiry body still streaming with water from the pool. 'But
I'm going to swim every day until I can too,' he declared
in a challenging manner. 'Come on, Juan!' and as if
time was of the essence he raced back to the pool with
Juan in hot pursuit.

Mary watching the boys begin a mock race, heard
Joan give a sigh before she said quietly, 'You can't
imagine how happy I am that Juan has someone of his
own age to play with.' She turned to look at Mary, her
hazel eyes serious now. 'He's been so very lonely, Mary.
We're quite a way out here, and although Pedro has
many friends, none of them live within reasonable
distance to us. Enrique will stay now, won't he?' she
asked anxiously.

Mary smiled back at her new-found friend. This appeared to be her morning for giving assurances, she
thought ironically. 'Yes,' she replied quietly, 'this is
his home, and this is where he belongs.'

Joan caught the underlying note of sadness in her
voice and gave her a searching look. 'But you don't,'

she said. It was a statement, not a question, and surprised Mary. She had no idea that her answer had been
so telling.

With her eyes on the boys now splashing each other,
Mary replied, 'Well, it's early days yet, of course, but
I honestly can't see where I fit in in these surroundings.'
She gave Joan a light apologetic smile. 'When all is
said and done, I'm a working girl, you know.' Her eyes
took in their immediate surroundings and the luxurious pool they were sitting beside, and she gave a light
shrug. 'It's just as if I were on holiday in one of those
luxurious hotels one reads about, but there's a time
limit attached to it.' Her smile widened as she added,
'I suppose I could become addicted to it given time,
but we shall have to see.'

'Oh, do try,' replied Joan, with a pleading note in
her voice. 'Believe me, I know exactly how you feel.
I felt the same when I first came here. Oh, not that my
home surroundings are half as grand as they are here,
but they're just as far removed from the semi-detached
house I was brought up in as, say, a crowded London
suburb.' She gave Mary an interrogative look. 'You do
come from London, don't you?' She then gave her an
apologetic smile. 'We talked of nothing else, you see,
for days after we heard the news. It was so wonderful
that after all this time Enrique's child should be found.
My Pedro isn't one to show emotion, but he was pretty
choked at the news, and when he saw young Enrique,
well——' she gave a sigh. 'According to him, it's just as
if Enrique had come back as a child again, the likeness
is so striking.' She smiled at Mary. 'He used to play with
Pedro when they were boys, you know, and I think
there's always some kind of a bond formed under those
sort of circumstances, don't you?' she asked gravely.

Mary nodded, not knowing what else to say. It was nice to know that someone else apart from Don Emilio wanted her to stay on, but it wasn't going to be as easy as that, not unless Rafael Alvarados removed his intimidating presence from the villa in the very near future. As for the mind-boggling conversation she had overheard the previous evening—she drew in a swift breath —maybe one day, when and if she ever got to know Joan well enough, she might be able to explain the reason why she was so certain that she did not belong there, and never would.

CHAPTER SEVEN

AFTER Mary had made Joan's acquaintance things were much easier for her and she was able to look forward to their meetings. Sometimes Joan would come over in the mornings with Juan, and the boys would spend most of the morning in the swimming pool with Enrique making a strong bid to outdistance Juan in the many races they challenged each other to, while she and Mary spent the time getting to know each other and indulging in local gossip.

On one occasion Mary went to Joan's home for morning coffee and sat in their sunny garden afterwards while the boys amused themselves either climbing the numerous fruit trees, or pretending to be bandits and skulking through the greenery, jumping out at intervals and uttering bloodcurdling yells that made Mary blink in astonishment the first time it happened, and made Joan chuckle at her reaction.

Invariably Rafael Alvarados's name would come up in the conversation, mainly because it was only on the occasions that Pedro came over to the villa to discuss business with Rafael that Joan was able to accompany him as she had sprained her ankle a week or so before Mary and Enrique's arrival, and as yet it was not strong enough for her to make the journey on foot as there was almost a mile between the two properties. There was no such problem for Mary, who had delighted in the walk to Joan's home, particularly as the route took her through the villa's garden and through an orchard that separated the properties.

It was now the weekend, and the bathing party Rafael had mentioned at the dinner party was to take place the following day. Mary, assuming Joan would be present, asked her what the party involved, mentioning that she was glad that there would be one person besides Don Emilio who could be relied upon to talk to her, whereupon Joan made a little moue with her wide generous lips and slowly shook her head. 'Oh dear,' she said with a grin. 'I'm afraid you'll have to rely on Don Emilio after all,' she frowned slightly, 'that's if he honours the occasion, he doesn't usually, he much prefers to stay in the shade with an informative book.'

At Mary's look of dismay she added quickly, 'Knowing Don Emilio, I shouldn't worry, Mary. He'll see that you're looked after.'

Mary wished she could echo these sentiments, for although she knew Don Emilio would do his best to see that she was entertained after what had happened at the dinner party she had no great hopes of his success. Her lips folded together firmly; in that case she would join him in the shade with a book of her own—she could always plead a headache—or that the heat was just a little too much for her. Don Emilio at least would understand this, and she didn't care whether Rafael Alvarados believed it or not. In all probability he would be relieved at her withdrawal from the scene. She had not seen much of him since the night of the dinner party, and only once had he honoured them with his presence at the dinner table, and then she suspected only at his father's insistence. His frequent absences were explained away by an apologetic and slightly embarrassed Don Emilio as duty calls on various friends. 'He has worked in London for almost two years now,' he told Mary, 'and rarely has the opportunity of seeing his friends. This is the longest stay he has made since he took over our interests abroad. I have no doubt that we shall see more of him when he tires of the social round. He is not much inclined to social gatherings, but no doubt he is mixing business with pleasure,' he had added philosophically.

With all her heart Mary wished she could explain to the kindly old man that he was not to feel embarrassed on her account for his son's disregard of social etiquette where she was concerned. She also fervently wished that she could tell him the reason behind his behaviour towards her, but without revealing the fact that she had overheard a certain conversation that would no doubt embarrass him far more than he already was by his son's diffident attitude, not to mention her feelings on the matter, she was powerless and had to remain silent.

There was another little side issue to consider too, and that was that she felt that Rafael was making sure that his father suffered from no illusion that he would eventually concede with his wish that he should propose to her, and this was his way of showing him that he had no intention of carrying out such a disagreeable task. If Mary was aware of this, so too must Don Emilio be, and until his departure probably in the near future, Mary could see no happy solution for either herself or Don Emilio.

Joan jerked Mary out of her silent reverie with a question. 'How many are going to be at this party, did they say?' she asked.

Mary shook her head. She wouldn't know any of the guests anyway, apart from the Alvarados's and Isabel, she said. At the mention of Isabel's name Joan's eyes widened slightly. 'So she's back, is she?' she said musingly. 'I thought she was in South America.' She gave Mary a knowing look. 'She must have heard that Rafael was home,' she added. 'I can't see her changing her plans for any other reason. It would also explain why we didn't receive an invitation,' she told Mary with a wry smile. 'We don't exactly get on,' she explained at the look of puzzlement she received from Mary. 'At least,' she added, 'Pedro has never liked her, quite apart from the fact that she treats us like servants —which we are—of course, but she has a way of making sure that you remain aware of the fact and don't attempt to rise above your station.'

'That I can well imagine,' said Mary quickly, remembering how she had been treated at the dinner party. She then recalled the conversation between Rafael and Don Emilio that had taken place after the dinner. 'She was engaged to Enrique, wasn't she?' she asked.

Joan gave her a surprised look. 'So you know about that, do you?' she replied, and shrugged. 'It's all so long ago and ought by now to be pushed into the archives, but that wouldn't suit our Isabel—not when she's still hoping to capitalise on it.'

'Where Rafael's concerned, you mean?' Mary queried without realising that she was showing more knowledge of the situation that she could possibly have learned in the short time that she had been there, and it was too late afterwards to wish that she had held her tongue.

'Did Don Emilio tell you this?' asked Joan with a trace of wonder in her voice.

Mary looked hastily away from her. 'Well, no——' she conceded slowly, and looked back at Joan wondering whether to tell her the truth of how she had ob-

tained the information and what she had overheard,
where Isabel was concerned, that was, but where she
was concerned it was much too personal to repeat even
to someone as sympathetic and as understanding as
Joan Santos.

Her mind made up, she related the event to Joan,
who gave her an appreciative grin as she imagined
Mary's discomfiture at finding herself an uninvited
eavesdropper on what was an exceedingly personal discourse between Don Emilio and his son. When she had
finished, Joan nodded in confirmation of what she had
said. 'It's true that Isabel has great hopes of Rafael
honouring Enrique's pledge,' she said musingly. 'According to Pedro, it was Rafael she really wanted and
she accepted Enrique's proposal out of pique.'

She was silent for a few seconds after this as she
thought back to that time. 'Pedro and I had just become engaged around then,' she went on. 'I do remember Pedro saying that Isabel would never make Enrique
happy.' She looked over the pool towards Juan and
Enrique's son now having a lighthearted argument
about something or other, and her expression softened.
'He was very fond of Enrique, as I've told you, and I
knew he wasn't happy about the engagement, particularly when the girl concerned was in love with his
brother Rafael.'

'Didn't Enrique know this?' queried Mary wonder-
ingly.

Joan shrugged her shoulders expressively. 'You've
seen Isabel,' she said dryly. 'There was never a lack of
suitors, and judging by the odd snippets of gossip,
nothing's changed, but there's only one Rafael Alvarados and she's not likely to accept anyone else while he
remains a bachelor. As for Enrique, he was as smitten

with her as the others that hung around her. He was too mesmerised by her beauty to see that she was using him to get at his brother. Leaving home was the best thing that ever happened to him. It gave him time to shake the stardust out of his eyes and see things as they really were. I honestly don't think he would have married Isabel, not after he had had a chance to think things out.'

Rafael would not have agreed with this supposition at all, thought Mary, and there was Don Emilio's strict code of honour to take into account as well. She spoke her thoughts aloud. 'I think you're forgetting Don Emilio, Joan, remember that Isabel is the daughter of an old friend of his.'

Joan gave another shrug at this. 'If Enrique had reached home,' she said slowly, 'and Don Emilio had heard about the child,' she gave Mary an apologetic smile, 'he would have been furious, yes, but he loved Enrique enough to bow to his wishes in this. It wasn't as if it was one of these accidental happenings. He really loved your sister.' She looked at the children and added thoughtfully, 'You know, I wouldn't be surprised if what happened wasn't deliberate. He must have known that it wasn't going to be easy extricating himself from his engagement to Isabel.' She gave a wry grimace. 'I can't imagine anything worse than being in love with someone and being forced to marry someone else, can you?' she asked Mary.

Mary wholeheartedly agreed with this; it was bad enough when you were heart-free, as she had good cause to know, and the thought of such a contract being formed between herself and Rafael Alvarados made her shudder.

'And to be perfectly frank,' went on Joan, 'what

you've just told me about Rafael's determined stand
to remain a bachelor somewhat eases my mind. I can
see a lot of changes coming if Isabel ever becomes mis-
tress here, and they wouldn't be in our favour. I know
she resents the easy relationship that exists between the
Alvarados's and Pedro's family, but as the children
were more or less brought up together such a relationship is bound to exist. Not,' she added hastily, 'that
Pedro ever takes advantage of this. He's turned down
many invitations on account of it. He knows his place,
and has no intention of overstepping the boundary between boss and foreman. He has his pride, too, you see,
and Señorita Isabel has a nasty way of stepping on that
pride. If Rafael did marry her, then we should have to
go, there would be no question of our staying on, Pedro
would not even consider it.'

From what Mary had seen of Rafael Alvarados she
could not imagine such a happening coming to pass
even if he did marry Isabel, not if he wished Pedro to
stay on as overseer, and she said as much, ending with,
'I simply can't see anyone changing his mind once it's
made up—not even his wife,' she announced forcibly,
unknowingly letting her feelings get the better of her.

Joan's brows lifted slightly at her vehemence. 'I
gather you don't get on,' she said with a smile, then was
serious again. 'Well, in that aspect you're quite right.
He's a law unto himself, and woe betide anyone who attempts to swerve him from his course. Even so,' she
added slowly, 'it would make things extremely awkward
all round—Pedro's dislike of Isabel is well known to
the family,' she grinned at Mary. 'That's why we didn't
receive an invitation to the swimming party, we
wouldn't have come anyway if we'd known she was going to be present. Not,' she added swiftly, 'that that

would have deterred Rafael from marrying Isabel if he'd a mind to do so, nothing would, but he's a proud man and would expect us to remain loyal to the family, and that's where the awkwardness would come in.'

Mary gave her a sympathetic nod. 'It would, wouldn't it,' she said slowly, then brightened. 'Well, you've no fear in that direction, not unless he suddenly has a brainstorm and falls under her spell, and somehow,' she tacked on with a twinkle in her eye, 'I can't see that happening, because although I don't much care for his personality, I think he can be relied upon not to lose his head, he prizes his freedom too much for that.'

The party began an hour after lunch, and Mary, not bothering to seek out Maria to see if she could provide her with a swimsuit, settled for a simple cotton dress and the inevitable straw hat, and wandered down to the pool with no great hopes of enjoying herself. One thing had pleased her though, and that was that even though Pedro and Joan would be absent, their son Juan would be present, and that meant that Enrique's time would be fully occupied. It also meant that Mary would find that she had to occupy herself in some other recreation as she had no intention of receiving another dose of thinly veiled insolence from either Rafael or Isabel.

Armed with a book on the history of old Seville, Mary advanced upon the party that was, she noted with some relief, a small gathering. Just Rafael and Isabel, and two young men, who at that moment were engaged upon a hot dispute on the merits of a certain matador and broke off the discussion on Mary's arrival.

After the introductions had been made, more for politeness' sake than for anything else, Mary felt that they really needn't have bothered, as apart from Isabel's

raised brows and, 'No swimsuit?' query, not even waiting for a reply, for her attention then turned towards
the boys who were shouting with laughter at something
that had amused them the other side of the pool, no
other attention was paid her, and she looked around
for Don Emilio, grateful for the small diversion that
had turned the spotlight away from her arrival.

Her hopeful look towards a shaded seat a little way
beyond the pool did not go unnoticed by the observant
Rafael. 'My father,' he told her with a slight derisive
note in his voice, 'will be joining us later.' His eyes
rested on the book she held in her hand. 'History of
Seville,' he said softly. 'How clever of you. It's my
father's favourite subject!'

Mary's cheeks flushed at the implied innuendo, and
she knew that it would be useless for her to point out
the fact that she was genuinely interested in the subject
and was not out to impress his father. Nevertheless her
pride made her reply sharply with eyes that flashed
with temper, 'I, too, have an interest in the past. I
hope to visit the Cathedral and other places of interest
while I'm here. It would be stupid of me,' she went
on, injecting what she hoped sounded like sweet reasoning in her voice, 'to pass up the chance, wouldn't
it?'

She saw his eyes narrow in speculation as he stared
at her, and it suddenly occurred to her that her words
must have sounded more like a threat than a reasonable
statement, and she hadn't meant them to.

'Thinking of leaving, are you?' he asked, his dark
eyes fixed on her flushed cheeks.

Mary was suddenly aware of the fact that she was in
the spotlight again as Isabel was now listening intently
to the conversation, while José and Carlos, the two

young men who made up the party, had stopped their
bantering conversation with the boys across the distance of the pool. Her colour heightened; really, it was
too much! Without even trying she had been put on
the defensive again. Oh, how she wished she could
leave then and there! though Don Emilio would have
something to say about that, and the thought of his re-
verting to a certain plan of his to keep her in Spain
made her reply hastily, 'In time, yes; but not until
things are settled here.'

Her words echoed in her brain as she realised with
horror that she had said the wrong thing again! She
knew exactly what Rafael Alvarados was thinking;
when she had received enough of a settlement to make
her departure worth while! The knowing smile of
derision she received from him proved her assumption
correct, and his softly said, 'Quite!' echoed his sentiments entirely.

Mary felt like waving a white flag; the opposition
was just a little too strong for her. The more she attempted to defend herself the deeper into the quagmire
she sank, and all she could do was to retire gracefully
from the combat. She chose a lounger that was not
being used, and placing her book on it started to pull
it away from the poolside and towards the shady spot
where a chair had been placed for Don Emilio's use.
It was within the vicinity, yet far enough away to in-
hibit conversation with the bathers, and as such was
ideal for Mary's purpose of bowing out of further in-
volvement.

'Let me do that,' said Rafael, with a note of sarcasm
in his voice, yet Mary was sure that he was relieved that
she was moving away from the pool and leaving the

party to enjoy themselves without the presence of an unwelcome stranger.

As Mary followed his tall form as he held the lounger aloft and went on ahead to place it beside the chair, she was acutely aware of his wide bare shoulders that glistened with the water from the pool, and as he turned towards her after he had put the lounger beside the chair, her eyes rested on his bare chest thick with black silky hair, the strands of which also glistened with drops of water and then down to the band of his trunks that fitted his slim waist. She was conscious of strength, of a masculinity that she had never encountered before, and it frightened her. She felt like the maiden aunt who got flustered at the very thought of entertaining a male to tea, be it the vicar or an old acquaintance. It was ridiculous, yet her fear was very real.

It was not until she looked up again at him that she realised that she must have been staring at him, and he was well aware of the fact by the very knowing look in his dark eyes as he gave her an abrupt nod and strode back to join his guests, leaving Mary feeling as if she had committed a cardinal sin.

With hands that trembled a little she settled herself down on the lounger and opened her book, determined to lose herself in it and escape from the confusion of her thoughts.

The opening paragraph was of no particular help to her in her heightened awareness of Rafael. 'How many stories of passionate and cruel love has Seville discovered?' read the introduction, and Mary felt the tears prick behind her lids but determinedly blinked them back, wondering if she had chosen the right book.

In spite of a reference a little further on that Seville

was Don Juan's city where he had lived his licentious life until he had a change of heart caused by an apparition, the book was all that she had hoped it would be, and gave details of fine sculptures to be found around the city, and a whole chapter devoted to the Cathedral and its treasures.

Lost in the descriptive literature, Mary did not at first hear Enrique calling out to her to witness the race about to be held between the boys and the men, who it appeared had challenged the boys to a race, and his indignant, 'Watch me, Madre!' at last pierced through to her, and she was forced to witness the event.

She was now wearing her sunglasses and she was grateful for the cover they gave her, enabling her to look in Rafael's direction without fear of his noticing the fact. She would have seen him anyway, as he stood next to Enrique, a tall towering figure against his nephew's slight one. Mary caught her breath; the likeness between them was indeed incredible, and she was sure that this fact had not escaped Isabel, now lounging as an onlooker by the side of the pool.

Enrique's son's arrival must have awakened bitter memories for her, Mary thought. Even though she had not loved Enrique, her pride must have taken a blow. Her thoughtful eyes rested on Isabel and the bright green bikini she wore that emphasised her lovely figure. Surely she ought to have been relieved that the engagement had been broken? Or had she not meant to go through with it anyway? Had she just used Enrique as an excuse to see more of Rafael, as Joan had said? Of course she had! Mary was utterly convinced of this. She had gambled on the chance of ensnaring Rafael before she honoured her pledge to Enrique. In any case, she would have found some good excuse as to why she

should delay the wedding. She had had no intention
of marrying Rafael's brother. Her fingers curled into
her palm; she was glad Enrique had found Sheila—even
though their love had such a short space of time to fulfil
itself. At least he had been happy—and so had Sheila.

A sudden shout and a loud splash told her the race
was on, and her attention went back to the swimmers.
As only one length of the pool was to be completed the
race did not take long, and Mary watched Rafael's easy,
almost languid crawl stroke overtake the rest of the
competitors. Juan was second, and Enrique just failed
to take third place from Carlos, with José coming in a
tired last.

Isabel's call of 'Bravo, Rafael!' reminded Mary that
she ought to congratulate Enrique on what was a
stupendous effort on his part, considering that he had
not been a strong swimmer and must have put in a lot
of practice to even compete! 'Well done, darling,' she
called, and felt Rafael's eyes on her as if in rebuke for
her enthusiastic comment.

Without her realising it her chin went up in a gesture
of defiance mixed with a certain amount of disdain,
and she turned her attention back to Enrique who
now stood with slightly hunched shoulders and jutting
bottom lip that told Mary that he was embarrassed by
her endearment. She sighed inwardly; he hated endearments, and she ought to have remembered this.
The trouble was, she thought sadly, she couldn't get
used to calling him Enrique, so if she had called, 'Well
done, Paul,' that would not have pleased him either!
This apparently was not going to be her day!

To Mary's vast relief Don Emilio joined them as refreshments were brought out to them. He walked
slowly and behind him, keeping at a respectable dis-

tance, came his manservant, intent on making sure that his master did not overtire himself, and ready to give assistance if required.

He was more than ready to sit down by the time he had reached Mary, but even so his panama hat was removed in courteous greeting to her before he sat down beside her.

As Mary accepted a cup of tea handed to her by a young maidservant, she saw that Isabel was now wearing a bathing wrap over her brief costume and assumed that she had taken the precaution of not offending Don Emilio's strict code of propriety.

There were soft drinks and delicious-looking cakes for the children, who fell upon the offered fare with gusto. Isabel had scorned the tea and settled for a long cold drink, as had the rest of the party, but Don Emilio joined Mary and partook the same beverage but without milk or sugar.

The fact that Mary sat apart from the rest of the party did not go unnoticed by Don Emilio, and his anxious frown as he asked solicitously, 'Not swimming, Mary?' showed his concern.

Refusing a dish of rich-looking pastries that had just been offered to her, Mary smiled at him. 'I'm not too sure about exposure to the sun as yet,' she told him. 'I felt it might be wiser if I did it gradually. I'm one of those unfortunate creatures that turn brick red under exposure, and I take ages to acquire a tan.'

She hoped he would accept her explanation, since it was the truth; she had a fair complexion that did not take kindly to sudden exposure. It still did not explain why she had elected to sit at a distance from the rest of the party, for most of the pool loungers had canopies. 'It looked so inviting here under the shade of the trees,' she tacked on hastily to forestall any further contemplation on Don Emilio's part.

The explanation appeared to have the desired result, and he nodded and smiled back at her. 'Very wise,' he commented thoughtfully in a way that told Mary that he was not heartily convinced of this, but was willing to accept it.

To Mary's pleasure Enrique and Juan came over to join them, each clutching a drink in one hand and a pastry in the other, and settled themselves solemnly on the grass beside Mary and Don Emilio's chairs.

That the children had elected to join their company gave both Mary and Don Emilio a lift of the heart. To Don Emilio, just to look upon the offspring of his son that looked so like his father, and to Mary, who had felt rather neglected these last few days by the child she looked upon as her own, the comforting knowledge that in spite of Enrique's newly acquired aplomb, she was still regarded as his property and this was his way of underlining the fact.

As before, Enrique was a little in awe of his grandfather, and Juan, mindful of the fact that Don Emilio was his father's employer, kept a respectful demeanour.

'Well, Enrique,' said Don Emilio, 'are you enjoying yourself?'

Enrique nodded emphatically in confirmation and hastily swallowed the last of his pastry, then stared up at his grandfather, his black eyes intent. 'How do you say "grandfather" in Spanish?' he asked solemnly.

The question pleased Don Emilio, who was about to give the translation when Juan, unable to contain himself said, '*Abuelo*!'

Enrique gave him an indignant look that plainly said, 'I was asking my grandfather, not you!' and Juan gave an apologetic grin and lapsed into silence again.

Don Emilio repeated the word, pronouncing it for Enrique's benefit. After several tries, and a chuckle from Juan, Enrique was able to pronounce it correctly, for which he received a nod of approval from the delighted Don Emilio.

'We must find a tutor for him,' the old gentleman said to Mary.

Mary's relaxed countenance now grew thoughtful. Was he to be taught at the villa, she wondered, or would he be sent to school? She sighed inwardly; there were so many things to discuss, but now was not the time.

'To teach me Spanish?' asked Enrique with a trace of pleading in his voice.

At Don Emilio's confirmation of this, he gave a whoop of joy and looked at Juan. 'Now I shall know what you are calling me,' he said triumphantly, but with an inflection in his voice that told Juan that he had better watch his step from now on.

A shout of laughter from the group by the pool drew their attention in that direction, and they saw José attempting a highly ambitious balancing trick with several glasses, and one that seemed doomed to failure as they watched the top section of the small pyramid he had built perilously wobble and then come tumbling down. An alert Rafael caught two of the glasses, and there was a mad scramble from Isabel and Carlos to retrieve the rest, amid much laughter.

This was too much for the boys, who unceremoniously took their leave of Mary and Don Emilio and rushed over to join the section where all the fun was going on.

As Don Emilio had not brought a book with him,

Mary did not attempt to read hers, particularly as she was mindful of a certain remark of Rafael's, and while Don Emilio's attention was still fixed on the revelry at the pool, she unobtrusively laid the book by the side of her chair and out of sight.

The rest of the afternoon passed pleasantly enough for Mary. With Don Emilio's company she felt less of an intruder, and with an ease she had never felt with anyone else she found herself relating events in the past that would be of interest to Don Emilio. But then he was interested in everything connected with her family, she realised with a spurt of surprise. With anyone else she might have felt embarrassed at discussing her personal affairs, but not with this kindly man. Before she knew it she found herself telling him about her previous worry of having to find another job at a reasonable distance from her home, and the reason why such a move would have been inevitable in time.

Don Emilio's understanding of the situation was shown by his later comment of, 'There is nothing so unsettling as the thought of someone waiting on the sidelines to fill your place. It always makes one strive that little bit harder, and the results are not always successful.'

Mary heartily agreed with this observation, knowing that in her case it was perfectly true. She had to be constantly on guard and not do or say anything that might bring recriminations on her head at a later date. She gave a sigh of relief at the thought that she was no longer under any such obligation.

As slight as the sigh had been, Don Emilio had caught it, and the underlying reason behind it, and gently patted Mary's hand. 'All that is over with now, Mary. Your future is here, to do as you wish,' and at her alarmed look at the thought of perpetual idleness, he gave a knowing smile. 'Don't worry about the future,' he told her gently. 'Things have a way of working out, you know. Just enjoy yourself and take what life offers.'

It was all very well, Mary thought afterwards, for Don Emilio to take a philosophical view of the future, but if he were still hoping to make a match between her and Rafael, his dreams were doomed to failure. José's balancing trick had had more chance of success than such a scheme!

CHAPTER EIGHT

THE following week Isabel came to stay at the villa for a few weeks, and Mary's heart had sunk at the news, since it meant that Rafael would not be departing for London as soon as Mary had hoped he would as it was inconceivable that Isabel would stay if he was away.

Although nothing was said Mary was sure that the arrangement had not pleased Don Emilio, but he was much too kindly a man to voice his feelings on the matter, for Isabel's father was visiting friends of his in South America and she had elected to stay in Seville.

The arrangement did not please Enrique either, for he resented Isabel's intrusion on the outings planned by Rafael where previously there had been only the two of them.

'She's sloppy!' he had declared to Mary in disgust after returning from a visit to meet some cousins of his who lived on the outskirts of old Seville, a visit that Mary had excused herself from on the excuse of wanting to catch up on her correspondence.

'What did you think of your cousins?' she asked to take his mind off his discontent.

'They're all right,' he replied in an offhand way, and refusing to be sidetracked continued with his complaints. 'She kept trying to hold my hand, and I wouldn't let her,' he stated with a glint in his eye that was soon replaced by a spark of appreciation as he remembered something else. 'Uncle Rafael told her I was perfeckly able to walk on my own,' he added in a satisfied tone. 'He let me sit beside him in the sports car, and she had to sit behind us,' he tacked on, a little maliciously to Mary's way of thinking. 'She didn't like that!' he declared happily.

Mary picked up the socks that he had discarded together with his shoes that he had left strewn over the bedroom floor as he prepared for his evening bath.

'How long is she going to stay?' he demanded after a short pause while he struggled with the buttons of his shirt.

She gave him what she hoped was a reproachful look. 'Only for a week or two, dear, so do try not to be rude to her. Remember she's your uncle's guest,' she told him as she rescued a button about to be torn from the material by the impatient Enrique.

'Well, I don't like her!' he declared emphatically, and gave Mary an indignant look. 'She's rude,' he stated. 'She keeps on interrupting when I'm talking to Uncle Rafael and asking questions, and,' he tacked on fervently, 'she doesn't like me. She makes out she does, but she doesn't!'

Mary sighed inwardly. It was unfortunately the truth; as Enrique resented her intrusion, so Isabel resented Rafael's interest in Enrique and was jealous of the attention afforded him. It was this that Enrique had spotted in the way that children had of uncannily seeing through all subterfuge. It was useless trying to fool them, as they had an inborn instinct for the truth.

'And I don't think Grandfather likes her either!' Enrique added for good measure.

'Now that's quite enough of that,' replied Mary firmly. 'You ought to take a lesson from your grandfather. He treats Señorita Isabel as a guest and is always polite, and so must you be.'

Muttering something under his breath about wishing his grandfather would throw her out, he left Mary to her ruminations and left for the bathroom.

As Mary listened to him splashing about in the bath with just a little more fervour than usual, she knew he was working off his feelings and her lips pursed in thought as she considered this new and most unwelcome development.

For the sake of peace she would have to go along on the next outing, that was going to be a visit to the coast and a day out on the beach. It was an outing she would have had to attend anyway, she thought wryly. Don Emilio was keeping a watchful eye on the situation and was not likely to accept another excuse from her as to why she should not accompany them.

Even without this added complication, she would not have looked forward to what ought to have been a pleasurable day on the beach, but in the company of Rafael Alvarados she had no such expectation. Now she would have to cope not only with his condescending attitude, but Isabel's supercilious one as well. Not to mention acting as a buffer between Isabel and Enrique!

Her soft lips twisted. It was just like old times, she told herself in an effort to cheer herself up. She had had plenty of practice in the past to undertake such a role, since the situation was identical to the one that had developed between Enrique and Derek.

She frowned as she went back to that time; children were possessive, of course, but in all fairness her opinion that Derek was mostly to blame for his stubborn and intractable attitude towards Enrique was unchanged. As an adult he ought to have known better, and made an effort to ease the situation instead of continually aggravating it.

Where Isabel was concerned, she decided to withhold judgment until she had had an opportunity of witnessing her behaviour towards Enrique. She sighed; there was no doubt that Enrique had taken to his Uncle Rafael in a big way and had formed a strong predeliction for his company, even to the extent of excluding Mary's company.

Under those circumstances it was natural for him to bitterly resent any intrusion that took his uncle's attention away from him, be it male or female, so perhaps, thought Mary, Isabel was not entirely to blame.

Another thought then crossed her mind and made her lovely grey eyes take on a bleak look. There was a possibility that Enrique had firmly established his uncle in the role of 'father', possibly without realising it, for Mary had not failed to note that he accepted without question any order that Rafael gave him, and it needed only a stern word to bring instant regret if he had misbehaved and an almost fervent wish to gain his uncle's approval again.

With anyone else she might have been worried over the possible repercussions such an alliance might bring about in course of time, but where Rafael Alvarados was concerned she had no worry, and that was strange considering the fact that she heartily disliked him.

The knowledge that she absolutely trusted Rafael Alvarados and was utterly certain that he would never cause Enrique a moment's concern over their relationship came as a slight shock to her, and the fact that her certainty had nothing to do with Don Emilio was even more of a surprise, but an oddly welcome one, as it meant that she would have no cause to worry over Enrique's future happiness. Don Emilio was old, and although the thought was not an enjoyable one, he could not live for ever, and Mary had at first kept this fact well to the fore as she tried to envisage Enrique's future in Spain, and a flow of relief flowed through her now at the thought that her fears had been groundless.

She would have no cause to worry over Isabel and Enrique either, for Rafael would be quite capable of handling any altercation that erupted between them.

When she went down to dinner that evening Mary was almost inclined to look kindly on Rafael. Now that Isabel was a guest he was duty bound to honour them with his presence at dinner, though it was hardly a duty, Mary decided, as she surreptitiously watched Isabel's playful yet purposeful attempts to hold his attention throughout the meal.

Whether it was Isabel's attendance at the meal, or whether it had been decided that Mary should sample a typically Spanish meal, she did not know, but as each course was placed before them Don Emilio took the trouble to enlighten her on the contents of the beautifully arranged dishes placed on the table. They consisted mainly of some kind of fish delicacies and were not, as Mary had previously assumed, highly seasoned, and she found herself enjoying her first adventure into the realms of the Spanish culinary art.

Isabel made no attempt that evening to converse in Spanish and even went so far as to actually address a question to Mary regarding England's inclement weather and how unfortunate the people were in having to put up with such short summers.

If it had been her intention to make Mary feel at ease in the company, the chosen subject was hardly a tactful one. In any case, she did not give Mary a chance to answer as she then turned her attention back to Rafael, making Mary wonder if she was really interested in the conversation or whether she was doing a little reconnaissance on Rafael's behalf regarding Mary's stated intention of returning home in due course.

'My poor Rafael!' went on Isabel, pouting her carmined lips at him. 'You've spent two years there. How relieved you must be to be back home again!'

Rafael's dark amused eyes rested briefly on her before he replied, 'I must agree it makes me appreciate my native land. What say you, Father? I seem to remember that you were not entirely enamoured of the vagaries of the English climate.'

Don Emilio's thoughtful eyes rested on his son but he parried a question to Mary before answering. 'And what, Mary, do you think of our summers?' He looked back at Rafael as Mary considered the question. 'If we are discussing extremes, then by all means let us not forget the effect our high temperatures must have on our visitors,' he told Rafael.

Mary was not sure whether she ought to break in at this point and heartily endorse Don Emilio's observances, but she sensed that he had set himself upon a course of championship in her defence and was quite capable of managing without her assistance.

'But that is only for four months of the year,' retorted Isabel, determined not to be left out of the conversation. 'And providing the visitor takes precautions I don't see that it need spoil their holiday,' she looked at Mary, 'but your summers are practically non-existent!' She gave an exasperated shudder. 'I was over there in June two years ago, and I don't think I've ever felt so cold,' she complained.

Mary smiled at this. 'If you were expecting to find the same temperature as you have here then you would have been disappointed,' she commented dryly. 'Even the temperatures of our good summers don't rise to these giddy heights. But then,' she went on slowly, 'it's what you're used to, isn't it? I must admit I felt completely drained for the first two days after I arrived, even though I did take the necessary precautions.'

Isabel gave her a look of thinly veiled dislike before answering smugly, 'Well, as you say, it's what you're used to. I wouldn't change our sunny climate for your chilly existence.'

'It's not always chilly,' answered Mary quietly, stung by her casual dismissal of her native land.

'Go on, Mary,' urged Don Emilio, sensing her indignation.

Mary looked away from him and down at the gleaming cutlery and the sparkling white damask cloth on the table in front of her, and then began to express her feelings. 'You see, I wouldn't change either. For one thing I would miss the spring.' Her lovely eyes held no animosity as she looked back at Isabel, she was too intent on her wish to express her feelings. 'I don't think there's any other country in the world that can rival my country at that time of year.' Her eyes held a pensive look in them before she went on. 'Then there's the autumn when the leaves of the trees turn to gold. It's a country of seasons that are always changing,' she nodded at Isabel's smirk. 'Oh, yes, we have rain and fog, not to mention snow and ice in the winter, but the seasons march on and soon it's spring again. Nothing stands still, you see.'

She turned to Don Emilio and gave him an apologetic smile. 'Although there are times when I must admit I've wished I were in a warmer climate, but even so, perpetual sunshine is just as foreign to me as a damp climate would be to you.' She turned her gaze back to Isabel again and vaguely noticed that she was not looking at her but at Rafael, and she doubted if she had heard one word. 'But, as I've said,' she ended lamely, feeling embarrassed now at holding forth at such length, 'it's just a question of what you're used to.'

If Mary's attention had not been intent on Isabel she would have seen that Rafael's eyes had never left her face while she had spoken. 'Spain, then, would not appeal to you as a permanent residence?' he asked.

Mary's eyes opened wide, and she felt rather than saw Don Emilio stiffen at the bald question. He was so determined to get rid of her, she thought indignantly, that he had not attempted to phrase the question a little more delicately—but then there was nothing delicate about Rafael Alvarados!

Her grey eyes clashed with the dark brooding ones still watching her closely, and her eyes held the distaste she felt for his obvious wish to remove her from Seville and making no pretence of his feelings on the matter. 'I thought I'd already made that quite clear,' she answered stiffly. She ought to have left it at that, but the wish to hit back at this autocratic man made her add pithily, 'Unfortunately Enrique is still at an age that requires a mother's presence, but believe me, I shall stay no longer than is absolutely necessary!' she declared emphatically.

There was a moment's silence after this uncharacteristic outburst of Mary's, and she closed her eyes as a feeling of contrition washed over her. How could she have let her feelings get the better of her? What must Don Emilio think of her? She swallowed and looked at him, but he was not looking at her but at Rafael, and his look spoke volumes and promised a confrontation in the not too distant future, and it was all so unnecessary, Mary thought wearily.

'Might I remind you that Mary is our guest, my son,' Don Emilio said in a tone that spoke of regret mingled with dignity. 'I'm sure that you did not mean to imply that she was not welcome here.'

'It's I who should apologise,' Mary broke in swiftly, not trusting Rafael to make an apology. 'The trouble is,' she said, giving Don Emilio a wan smile, 'that I'm much too independent, I've had to be in the past, and to suddenly find myself in this sort of position is irksome.' Her eyes pleaded with Don Emilio to understand. 'You must remember you once had occasion to remark on this attitude of mine.'

Mary's ploy in wishing to avoid any further unpleasantness was successful, and the rest of the dinner passed off in a more normal if not completely harmonious atmosphere.

After coffee had been taken in the lounge Mary's hopes of escaping to her room were forestalled by Don Emilio suggesting a game of bridge, or some such similar game that all were acquainted with. It was a good suggestion, Mary acknowledged, as the undertone of her clash with Rafael still hovered about them, but Isabel had no intention of spending the evening staring at a pack of cards when there was a chance of a tête-à-tête with Rafael, no doubt to sympathise with him on the outspokenness of the English girl, Mary thought ironically.

It was then settled that Mary should play cards with Don Emilio, and Isabel and Rafael engaged themselves upon a board game that required little concentration apart from the throwing of the dice.

As Chinese patience was the only game that Mary

could play with confidence, it was the game chosen by
Don Emilio, who Mary suspected would have played
Snap with her if that had been the limit of her ex-
pertise with cards, such was his obvious wish to make
up for her discomfort at dinner.

Although there was a certain amount of concentration required for their game, loud shrieks from Isabel
every now and again pierced through the silence and
would inevitably draw Mary and Don Emilio's attention towards her and Rafael.

On one occasion after a particularly boisterous ex-
change between them, Mary saw Don Emilio frown and
give what she could only discern as a puzzled look towards their table, and before long she was able to understand his bewilderment, for there was no doubt at
all that Rafael was deliberately encouraging Isabel's
high spirits and engaged upon what might be termed
as a 'flirtatious fling' with her.

For a man who had emphatically declared that he
had no interest in the lady concerned he was acting
rather out of character, Mary thought, and so apparently did Don Emilio.

When a little later Isabel commented on the close-
ness of the atmosphere in the room and suggested a
walk in the garden to Rafael, even Mary was surprised
when Rafael fell in with this suggestion without the
slightest hint of reluctance, and as she watched them
go through the french windows she stole a look at Don
Emilio also watching them and felt a pang of sympathy
for him as she noted the exasperation and sheer annoyance his son's behaviour was causing him.

She did not think that he was worried over the possibility of Rafael going back on his word, although his
behaviour towards Isabel that evening certainly sug-

gested that he might be seriously considering it. If it came to a choice between Isabel and a Miss Allis, then the odds were very definitely in Isabel's favour, she thought with an inward smile, and that was something to be thankful for from her point of view.

It was not long after Rafael and Isabel had left for their walk that Don Emilio asked Mary if she would mind if they made this the last game, and she willingly agreed, not feeling too happy at the tiredness he had shown during the last two hands. A stab of remorse flowed through her at the thought of her outburst at dinner; if she had only held her temper it would have saved Don Emilio much embarrassment, but it was too late now to call back those angry words, for although he had accepted her swift intervention to prevent further trouble, she knew that he was fully aware that Rafael had been the instigator of the flare-up and that it must have hurt his pride to accept her hastily thought up excuse to keep the peace.

How could Rafael have placed his father in such an embarrassing position? Mary wondered as she undressed and prepared herself for bed. There was no doubt that he genuinely loved his father, yet on the subject of one Mary Allis he was as immovable as a stone wall, and had no compunction whatsoever in defying his wishes, making it patently clear that he had no time for her, guest or no guest!

She was now back to disliking Rafael with a stronger intensity than before, and felt that Enrique had let her down badly by taking such a liking to the wretched man. How she was going to spend a whole day in his company after what appeared to be a declaration of war on both sides was beyond her.

Confused images floated through her drowsy mind as

she tried to envisage what the following day would bring, and she found herself wondering how her Enrique would shape up as a peacemaker should her temper get the better of her. It was strange, she thought just before she dropped off to sleep, she had never lost her temper with Derek; she had been exasperated, yes, but always in command of her emotions, but there was something about Rafael Alvarados——

The following morning Mary waited apprehensively outside the villa with Enrique shortly after seven o'clock, for the journey would take several hours and an early start was essential.

When they heard the purring of an engine being started up behind the villa, Mary looked round for Isabel, but the large ornate doors of the residence remained shut and she wondered what kind of a mood Rafael would be in if he had to wait until Isabel deigned to put in an appearance.

A few seconds later the large car slewed to a standstill beside them and firmly ensconced in the front seat sat Isabel, deceptively casually dressed in a lemon silk trouser suit, her dark hair caught up in a chignon of matching colour, making Mary wonder a little maliciously what time she had got up that morning to present such a picture of femininity.

Enrique's gasp of indignation at the sight of Isabel sitting in the front seat was not lost on Mary, who gave an inward sigh of dejection. This was only the start, she told herself, and it promised to be a day to remember, but not for its enjoyable attributes!

As they started to get into the car, Isabel patted the front seat between Rafael and herself and smiled at Enrique. 'Come and sit beside me,' she requested royally, somehow making the gesture a condescension on her part.

Enrique looked back at Mary and then at the front seat, and that look said more than words. He would sit in the front providing Mary sat beside him.

Although applauding his preference for her company Mary felt that he was rather overdoing it, 'I'm perfectly happy to sit in the back,' she told him firmly. 'You'll see much more if you sit in the front,' she urged him gently.

'So will you!' stated Enrique just as firmly, and followed Mary into the back seat not even bothering to say, 'No, thank you,' to Isabel's offer.

Shades of his Uncle Rafael, Mary thought darkly as the car swung down the drive and out on to the main road.

In spite of a sulky Enrique and a too-cheerful Isabel who did not bother to waste words on either Mary or the child, but directed all conversation to the man by her side, Mary was completely enthralled by the different aspects of the scenery in Spain.

They passed barren land dried by the exposure of the sun, and would then suddenly come across luxuriant vineyards. These were replaced by olive groves as they travelled across the uplands that gave magnificent views of hazy blue mountains in the distance. By the time they had stopped at a tourist refuge for refreshments it was mid-morning, and Mary, attending to Enrique's requirements, felt decidedly lightheaded, and she vaguely wondered if it was possible to be intoxicated with an overdose of magnificence! Such an impact had the scenery had upon her. Harsh and unrelenting in the barren areas that would suddenly switch to a land of milk and honey, and before you could assimilate the change of landscape the savage beauty of the mountains was clamouring for your attention. It brought home to Mary the vastness of the country that she was visiting whose moods were as variable as those of a temperamental woman.

She dragged her eyes away from the snow-capped mountains that loomed up in front of the small inn where they sat taking their refreshments, and then looked down at the small villages nestling on the hillsides below them. She could find no words to express her feelings of the sheer exuberance that flowed through her veins. She was content just to look and absorb the grandeur of the scene, and as with the fountain at the villa she felt that she could stay there for ever and never tire of the view.

Rafael directed Enrique's attention to a team of mules climbing up a distant mountain, and from that distance they looked like a column of ants on the march. As Mary saw them move to the edge of the plateau for a clearer view, she saw Isabel rush to join them and gave a sigh of exasperation. Surely she did not begrudge the child just a few moments alone with Rafael? But apparently she did, and Enrique's swift change of expression on her intrusion could not have been lost on someone as perceptive as Rafael, thought Mary, and felt a little stab of justification as she saw Rafael direct a distinctly chilling look at Isabel that might have had an impact on a less determined person, but went seemingly unnoticed by her. Either she was completely insensitive, or so dead set on her goal to capture Rafael as a husband that she was immune to all else, and Mary was inclined to think that it was the latter.

The rest of the afternoon passed in what might have

been an idyllic way had it not been for the fact that
Enrique and Isabel continually vied for Rafael's attention. Mary, having changed into a demure one-piece
costume after they had arrived on the surprisingly un-
crowded beach of the coastal resort, lay back and
watched the interplay feeling curiously detached from
the gambits adopted. It made a change for her to stand
on the sidelines and watch battle commence without
having to continually attempt to smooth things over
as she had had to do with Enrique and Derek.

Even, she thought, if she had been inclined to act as
a buffer between the parties and made some definite
attempt either to direct Enrique's attention or Isabel's
from their desired goal of holding Rafael's interest, it
would not have worked, and she would have received
no thanks from Rafael for what he would have termed
her interference.

Having had some experience of the part now desig-
nated to Rafael, who must be fully aware of the tactics
employed by his nephew and Isabel to gain his attention, Mary had to concede that he was doing very well
without her assistance. She assumed that he was well
used to being the centre of attraction, and no wonder,
she thought as her eyes lingered on his tanned lithe
body as he relaxed on the sands between Enrique and
Isabel.

There was nothing puny about Rafael Alvarados, she
decided; there was strength in every line of his body,
and in some way his strength reminded her of the
mountains that could still be seen hovering in the distance. Their moods of beauty and savagery were in her
mind closely aligned to the man who was Enrique's
uncle. He, too, could be gentle with those he loved,
but as savage and as terrifying as an avalanche against

those he considered his foes.

Mary shivered at the thought and then shook herself out of her fanciful musings. No wonder the Spanish were a proud race, their heritage was steeped in history, a history as turbulent and as awe-inspiring as the country itself, mused Mary as she recalled the drive down the mountainside when the car seemed to take wing as it hurtled down the pass towards the resort, and how even Enrique had forgotten his grievances and had shouted for sheer joy at the exhilaration of the experience.

As the warmth of the sun caressed her bare shoulders, Mary lay back and removing her sun-glasses, she closed her eyes and relaxed in utter contentment. She thought of the letter that she had received from Sarah in reply to her request that she keep an eye on Mary's house until such time as she could return, either to stay or to wind things up, and to find herself another job and possibly a flat to live in near whatever job she had been able to obtain.

At no time had she envisaged herself accepting Don Emilio's offer of staying permanently in Spain, not even if Rafael Alvarados returned to England and made the spasmodic returns to his home in Seville that judging by Don Emilio's remarks had been few and far between in the past.

Sarah had been delighted that 'Paul' had settled down so happily, but mentioned that Michael was missing him, particularly as it was the summer holiday period. She had told Mary not to worry about anything, she would keep an eye on the house and water her geraniums in the kitchen for her. The letter had left Mary with a glow of gratefulness for the kindness of Sarah Holland, and she was thankful that she had left the keys of the house with her before her trip to Spain.

She must not leave it too long, she thought, before she settled her affairs in London. Not now that Enrique's future was settled and he would not be returning to England with her. She would have to stay in Spain, of course, until she was sure that he did not need her constant presence. On this thought she bit her lower lip. It could be years, or months, who knew? How could you measure such things? Mary couldn't, and she doubted if anyone else could.

The only thing she did know for certain was that she would not be needing a three-bedroomed house any longer, and that her life had changed out of all proportion from what she had expected. To the loneliness in front of her she resolutely closed her mind; time enough to think of that when it came.

To turn her mind to other matters she glanced across towards Enrique and saw that he was listening with rapt attention to something that Rafael was telling him, and she caught snatches of the conversation. He was relating how once he and Enrique's father had taken a mule trip into the mountains. As she listened to his deep voice she thought how perfect his English was, and if she had half the command of the Spanish language that he had of her native tongue, she would be well satisfied.

Her thoughts then turned to Rafael's brother and the fact that he had to have extra lessons to improve his English, and she wondered why then she vaguely remembered Don Emilio mentioning the fact that his younger son had not had robust health when a child, and this, she thought, had probably held up his education.

As if her thoughts were communicated to Isabel,

who was now picking up handfuls of sand and letting the golden grains slip through her scarlet-nailed fingers, she said something in rapid Spanish too fast for Mary to translate, but whatever it was it showed her impatience at their immobility, closely aligned, Mary thought sardonically, with the fact that Enrique was receiving more attention than she was.

Rafael went on with his narration, but it ended shortly after Isabel's intervention, and Enrique, who felt that he might have said more but for her remarks, turned towards her. 'I did not understand what you said,' he stated coldly, and for all his age and slight stature his words held a ring of autocratic censure that made Mary swallow hastily to prevent a chuckle from escaping. Was this her Paul? she thought in wonderment.

The fact that Rafael had taken due note of his nephew's censure of Isabel's impatient intrusion into the conversation was shown by a slight twitch of his firm lips and a look of—what? mused Mary; could it be approval?—in his dark eyes as they rested on Enrique.

Isabel's eyes flashed as they went from Rafael to Enrique, then she shrugged and addressed Rafael as if to say she had not been talking to Enrique anyway, and spoke again in Spanish, and this time Mary understood what she was saying. 'Why do we sit here when we could be swimming? You have plenty of time to reminisce about the past. Not that I want to remember. I'm still trying to forget,' she ended pettishly, glancing up at Rafael from under her dark thick lashes and giving him a helpless pleading look.

'Speak in English, Isabel,' Rafael said gently yet firmly, 'then we shall all understand you.'

Isabel gave him a look that spoke plainly of her disappointment at his refusal to play a game of passing comments on to one another that excluded the present company, but nevertheless she obeyed his order. 'I was merely suggesting we take a swim,' she said to Enrique, only remembering Mary's presence as an afterthought and looking towards her. She then turned back at Rafael. 'I'll race you to that platform,' she said challengingly.

Mary followed her glance towards a diving platform a little way out in the bay, and although she could not judge its exact distance she knew that it was further than the length of the swimming pool at the villa. With this thought in mind she was considerably alarmed to see that Enrique had every intention of taking part in the race that Isabel had obviously only expected Rafael to participate in.

'If we go along the beach,' Mary said swiftly to Enrique, 'we can watch the race and see who wins,' she suggested hopefully, and gave Rafael a pleading look. He surely would not allow him to take part in the race, and the stubborn set of Enrique's chin told her that only his uncle could prevent him; he would not listen to her.

If Rafael saw the look he did not acknowledge it, but patted Enrique's head with a gesture of approval. 'Very well, Enrique, I shall pace you, and haul you on to my back if you tire.' He gave the now fuming Isabel an amused look and then looked back at the twice-as-tall Enrique glowing with pride at his uncle's confidence in his swimming prowess. 'Are you ready?' he asked with a note of amusement in his voice.

Mary watched them wade out until the water was deep enough for them to start the race, then take off in their different styles. Rafael, with a slow lazy crawl, paced as he had said to match Enrique's snatched strokes at the crawl style that must be more exhausting than the actual stroke because of his effort to make progress without completing the arm strokes that would give him the speed he desired.

Isabel, Mary saw, favoured the breast stroke and was on a par with her own swimming proficiency that was not particularly outstanding, and Mary was grateful that she had not been invited to join the race, as she would have had to refuse. The sea held no attraction for her, because she had had a near escape when she was a child and had been carried out to sea on a rubber lilo. It was an experience she had never forgotten and had no wish to repeat, and she had since confined her activities to the safety of a swimming pool.

Really, thought Mary, as she watched the now tiring Enrique being hauled on to Rafael's back half-way to the target yet still ahead of Isabel, she might not have been present, and she wondered if anyone would notice if she just wandered off on her own pursuits. She felt just like a nanny asked to accompany a family to keep an eye on the children, yet should she adopt this role she knew that Rafael Alvarados would take exception to it. Look how he had completely ignored her silent plea not to let Enrique take part in the race—and so it would be with any other wish of hers, and not only where Enrique was concerned.

She thought of his attitude towards her that day, that had been one of silent yet watchful observation, making her wonder just what she was expected to do or say that would mar the enjoyment of the day for them. When she recalled her outburst at dinner the previous evening she was not really surprised at his attitude, and was a little sorry that he was going to be disappointed in his expectancy that she would again let her feelings get the better of her common sense, and in his eyes show herself up for the self-seeking, mercenary type that he had labelled her.

At this point the swimmers reached the platform, Rafael and Enrique just ahead of Isabel, and Mary's thoughtful eyes watched as Rafael lifted Isabel out of the water with an effortless action and placed her on the wooden boards. Did he hold her a little longer than was strictly necessary, she wondered, or had Isabel clung on to him? Mary's lips twisted—not that it was any business of hers, he could marry her for all she cared. At this thought her smooth forehead creased suddenly. No, she did not want Rafael to marry Isabel because if he did Enrique's position would be just as precarious as it would have been if she had married Derek, from the happiness point of view if not from the material, and it was happiness Mary wanted for Enrique. Money could ease many situations, but it counted for nothing against the blessing of happiness.

A nasty thought then entered her reasoning; did Rafael have some thought in mind of relieving her of her responsibilities by taking a wife? The thought made her bite her lower lip in anxious worry. He would be quite capable of taking such an action to gain his target in removing her as soon as possible from the scene.

On recalling his reaction to Don Emilio's suggestion that he propose to her her heart beat faster in agitation. It might well have planted the seed of thought in his mind. Enrique still needed a mother's care and would turn to Mary until he was old enough to spurn such maternal guidance. He must also, she thought miserably, have taken this into consideration, and must have been just as aware as she herself had been that it could take several years. She was not unmindful of the fact that such a thought must have been extremely distasteful to him, since it would mean her constant presence in Seville.

Her worried eyes rested on the small group on the diving board now stretched out relaxing in the sun, and as Enrique waved at her she returned the wave, glad that he was not near enough to see the misty gathering in her eyes at the thought of what the future might hold for both of them.

By the time they had returned to the beach Mary had convinced herself that Rafael would marry Isabel. He would not concern himself with the fact that Isabel and Enrique did not get on —or if he had, he would have assured himself that given time things would work out to a satisfactory conclusion. Isabel would do what he told her to do; typically Spanish, she knew her place in the home, but what about the times when Rafael was away on business? How would Isabel and Enrique fare then? There was Don Emilio, of course, but this thought gave her little comfort; Don Emilio would not always be there to see fair play.

On the return journey Mary was so quiet that even the excited Enrique, exhilarated because he and Mary had been allotted the front seat for the homeward run, noticed her reticence and asked her, 'You don't feel sick, do you?'

At this solicitous query Mary's despondency lightened and she had to give a little smile as she replied that she was quite well and not liable to ask for the car to be stopped at some convenient spot, as had been the case on past occasions when Enrique had overindulged in an orgy of ice creams when a similar trip had been taken.

After this little interlude Mary was left to her miserable musings again, and this time she was left in peace.

CHAPTER NINE

FROM then on Mary made a point of observing Rafael's attitude towards Isabel to try and ascertain whether her suspicion that Rafael would propose to the other girl was correct.

As the days went by and Mary attended every outing planned by Rafael for the enjoyment of his guests, she was forced to come to the conclusion that if he had not already made up his mind, he was certainly considering it.

Not that there was anything she could definitely pin down in terms of extra affection from him to Isabel, it appeared to be all on Isabel's side, but then he was not a demonstrative man, Mary decided, and was just as likely to casually ask Isabel to marry him as sweep her into his arms and demand her acceptance of his proposal.

Whether it was because she was more attentive to his different moods, or because she was on the alert for any change in his behaviour towards Isabel, she soon became aware of receiving the same amount of scrutiny from the man she was surreptitiously watching.

At first she was inclined to think that she had imagined his silent attentiveness to her presence, whether she was just sitting listening to the conversation or attending to Enrique's wants, but an incident that took place not long after she had become aware of his scrutiny soon proved beyond all doubt that it was not her imagination but a disturbing fact.

It happened while they were visiting the Cathedral; a visit Mary had been longing to make, but had hoped to be alone and able to absorb the age-old atmosphere without the vexing presence of Rafael and Isabel, not to mention a bored Enrique who could barely contain his impatience as the next stop on the agenda was to be the bullring and he had no intention of overstaying the Cathedral visit in favour of such a treat.

There was so much to see, so much to try and take in, and although Mary tried she knew full well that it would take several visits to do the Cathedral justice. A quick walk round and a few observances about this and that was of no use to Mary. She wanted to linger and to wonder at the rich tapestries, to gaze at the glorious paintings painted by masters of the art, and to hear the sombre but beautiful masses being said in the numerous chapels of the vast building that not only formed the perfect background setting but enriched and enhanced it.

When Enrique asked for the third time if it was time to go, Mary felt a stab of disappointment, and the thought of their next stop made her say to Rafael, 'Please go on. Perhaps I could meet you all later?'

To her delight and relief Rafael agreed to her proposal, and suggested that they all meet later outside the Cathedral, asking with what she was surprised to note was a suspicion of a twinkle in his dark eyes if she thought an hour would be long enough for her, and on receiving her grateful nod left her to continue her exploration.

The time flew by, but Mary was unconscious of it; there were many tourists visiting the Cathedral and each party had a guide, and sometimes she would linger on the edge of the gathering and listen to the guide relating a particular piece of history regarding a certain relic.

It was at one of these times when the deep voice of Rafael cut into her absorption in Christopher Columbus's tomb after the party she had temporarily joined had left.

Mary's start and unconcealed dismay at his reappearance at what seemed to her to be a short time after his departure did not go unobserved by him. 'Perhaps,' he said, 'I should have made it two hours!'

Her eyes met his, not certain whether he was annoyed with her, or if he was just passing a general comment, but she could detect no annoyance in his eyes, only that same still watchfulness that she had become aware of.

'Have you finished?' he asked with slightly lifted brows, 'or is there something else you would like to see?'

It was all Mary could do not to gape at him. He was actually trying to please her and this was a new experience for her; she swallowed quickly and to cover her embarrassment looked around for Enrique and Isabel.

'I have left Enrique sampling an ice with Isabel,' he told her, proving that he was aware of her discomfort and, she suspected, deriving some amusement from the fact. 'They are quite capable of entertaining themselves,' he added softly.

Mary had come out of her surprised state and was now slightly wary of the change in Rafael's manner towards her, and the phrase of 'if you can't beat them, join them,' hovered around her bemused mind. Even if there had been something she had particularly wished to see, this new development would have completely driven it out of her mind. 'No, thank you,' she found herself saying, and looked round wildly for the exit, having a sudden longing for Enrique and Isabel's company.

Rafael, however, was not so easily discouraged. 'Your interest is pleasing,' he said quietly. 'I am as proud of our heritage as my father is. It would be no hardship to me to escort you to whatever part of the Cathedral you wish to visit.' His eyes lingered on the beautiful stained glass windows ahead of them. 'The paintings alone are worth a second visit,' he added slowly, then gave her a slow heart-stopping smile. 'Perhaps you are right. I shall make a point of ensuring that you have more time on your next visit.'

'Thank you,' was all Mary could find to say in her confusion at the sudden switch of attention that Rafael was affording her.

'We're going to see a bullfight,' announced Enrique as soon as Mary joined them, and at her look of utter consternation Rafael intervened with, 'Not today, to-morrow. The ladies may be excused, of course.'

'But I adore bullfights,' complained Isabel, giving Rafael an accusing look. 'You know I do! Please include me in the treat,' she begged him pleadingly.

'Very well,' replied Rafael, but Mary could tell that he was not pleased with her. Neither was Enrique, if the scowl on his face was anything to go by!

'Girls don't like that sort of thing,' he said darkly yet hopefully.

'I am not a girl!' answered Isabel acidly. 'I'm a *señorita*. Surely you've learnt that much? And *señoritas* like bullfights,' she added pithily, then turned back to Rafael, dismissing Enrique's indignant reply to her scathing remark on his Spanish as if it were of no consequence. 'You didn't think I would want to miss such an oportunity, surely? Remember how we used to queue for hours when we were young?' she reminded him, adding on a sad note, 'There seems to be much that you have forgotten.'

Rafael answered her in their native tongue, and it was the first time that he had used Spanish in Mary's and Enrique's company, but it proved to Mary that his patience with Isabel was wearing a little thin. Although he spoke rapidly, Mary was able to gather the gist of his words, and they were not at all loverlike or complimentary to Isabel. He told her in no uncertain terms that there were times when the feminine element was not required, and this was one of them, and for that simple reason he had arranged to spend the afternoon with his nephew.

The quick flush in Isabel's cheeks told Mary that she had taken the point, but nevertheless resented it. She did not, however, bow out of the visit as Mary would have done in the same circumstances, but replied sharply that she would be sure to find some friends there, and if that was what he wanted then she would sit elsewhere.

After this short but highly instructive altercation between Rafael and Isabel, Mary began to have second thoughts about the probability of Rafael marrying Isabel.

As pretty as Isabel was, she was also thoroughly spoilt, and had no intention of taking second place to anyone, even begrudging a child a few hours' privacy with his uncle.

On the way back to the villa Mary sat with the still fuming Isabel in the back of the car, while Enrique lorded it in the front seat beside his uncle. There was something about his dark upright-held head that told

Mary that he was well pleased with the turn of events. He did not understand Spanish, but the look in his uncle's eye when he had spoken to Isabel was proof enough for Enrique that Isabel had been well and truly put in her place. If he had had any doubts on this, her furious response would have soon dispelled them.

She was not, Mary thought, being very clever; if she had stopped to think about things she would have realised that she was not helping her cause one little bit by these shows of tantrums, for that was what they really amounted to. Everything was fine as long as she received what she considered was her due accolade from whatever company she was in, but woe betide anyone who attempted to put her in the shade.

Even while condemning Isabel's attitude, Mary was able to partially understand it. She knew that the Spaniards revered beauty in any form, and there was no denying that Isabel was beautiful. She must have grown up with an exalted opinion of herself at the many highly complimentary remarks she would have received from the appreciative male population, who would not have stinted their admiring comments.

When Mary recalled that Rafael's brother had wanted to break off their engagement, it was not hard to imagine Isabel's fury—and it would have been fury, not sorrow, Mary presumed. Her attitude towards Enrique's son had supported Joan Santos's assumptions that she had had no intention of going through with the marriage, not while Rafael was unattached and there was still a chance of ensnaring him.

Isabel's air of affronted dignity during dinner that evening made the meal an uncomfortable one for Mary, for she found herself once again receiving attention from Rafael and this only served to annoy Isabel further.

Don Emilio was not present at the meal, and Mary, remembering how tired he had looked that morning, was not surprised to learn that he had retired early. She sorely missed his comforting presence particularly as she was still trying to assimilate Rafael's sudden change of attitude towards her, and wondered what Don Emilio would make of it.

Her thoughtful grey eyes rested on Rafael's strong profile as he turned to answer a coquettish remark of Isabel's, who must have come to the belated conclusion that her doleful air of wounded dignity was not having the desired effect upon Rafael, and was in fact, directing his attention to Mary.

After dinner Mary decided to go to bed at the earliest given opportunity. Without Don Emilio's company she could only envisage a miserable evening on the receiving end of Isabel's sharpened talons as her sudden recovery of spirits had not had the desired effect either, and Rafael had continued to favour Mary with his attentions.

If Mary was having trouble trying to absorb this puzzling turn of events in her favour, how was Isabel, for she had never envisaged Mary as a rival for Rafael's affections. At this thought Mary nearly choked as she drank her coffee. Whatever else she might be rivalling Isabel for it was certainly not Rafael's affections, and she wished fervently that she knew what he was up to. He had some plan in mind, that much was certain, for men like Rafael Alvarados did not suddenly alter their opinions, and his opinion of Mary had not been what one might term as inspired.

As soon as she had drunk her coffee, Mary chose what

she hoped would be an advantageous time to make her departure as Isabel was holding Rafael's attention by getting him to unravel a thread of silk from her shawl that had become entangled on her bracelet, and saying a hasty 'goodnight' she made her way to the door.

She had barely reached the door when Rafael's smooth voice cut off her retreat. 'I hope you are not leaving us, Mary. I particularly want to talk to you.' He gave the open-mouthed Isabel a warning look before he added, 'I'm sure Isabel will excuse us if we take a stroll in the garden. You might like to entertain Father for a little while,' he suggested to the amazed Isabel.

Mary's confused mind tried to come up with a few excuses as to why she would not be able to accept his, to her sensitive feelings, ominous invitation, but she was well aware that whatever excuse she came up with it would not serve to distract him from his course. She swallowed and found herself inclining her head in agreement, steadfastly avoiding Isabel's furious eyes.

'You might collect a wrap of some sort,' he told Mary, and gave an ironic smile as he added, 'but please, I beg you, not of the lacy variety, they are apt to cause diversions.'

Mary might have reminded him that she wore no bracelets, but if the truth were to be told she would probably welcome some diversion, she told herself as she went to her room to collect a cardigan.

By the time she rejoined Rafael and entered the garden with him, she had convinced herself that he had decided to offer her money to precipitate her early removal from Seville. To her way of thinking it was the only reason why he had changed his tactics and adopted a 'be kind to Mary' attitude.

There must have been something in her quiet ac-

ceptance of the situation that she had found herself in
during the few weeks that she had been resident in the
villa that had made him decide to bring matters to a
head, she thought, as she waited in silence for him to
make whatever offer he thought would meet her approval.

'There is a quietness about you, Mary Allis, that is
extremely disturbing,' he began, throwing Mary out of
her bitter musings and into a state of panic at the
thought that he might be using flattery to enable him
to gain her support for what he had in mind. 'And I
must admit,' he went on in that deep voice of his, 'that
at the start of our acquaintance I had not formed a very
good impression of your character.' At this Mary's hands
clenched at her side. He was talking about the conversation he had overheard between Derek and herself, and
although she had to admit that on the face of things it
must have looked as if she was out to gain recompense
for bringing up Paul.

'Since then, however,' he continued slowly, 'I have
altered my previous opinion.' He stared down at the
silent Mary, whose pale oval face was quite visible in
the creamy light of a large moon. 'You are either an
extremely clever scheming woman or an exceptionally
attractive one.' At Mary's gasp at this bald observance,
he added, 'I prefer to think of you as the latter. If I
am wrong,' he hesitated here and then went on, 'either
way, you will have nothing to fear from the future as
far as you and Enrique are concerned.'

They continued walking down the narrow path that
led to the lower gardens and Mary wondered whether
he expected her to thank him for this assurance for
their future. For Enrique's future, she reminded herself, for if Rafael attempted to offer her some monetary

recompense he would soon find which of his two earlier observances was the correct one!

In the event she remained silent, sensing that he had more on his mind than just assuring her of their future.

'What I am now about to ask you may seem preposterous, but I would ask you to bear in mind the fact that my father's health, although much improved, holds out no hope of longevity. It is for this reason that I have decided not to return to England, but to appoint a manager to take over our affairs in London. There is also,' he went on slowly and deliberately, 'the undeniable fact that Enrique needs a mother's guidance and will do for several years to come.' His eyes bored into Mary's as he added, 'Taking all these things into consideration I have come to the conclusion that I must take a wife. I am asking you if you will do me the honour of accepting my proposal.'

At that moment Mary was incapable of accepting anything, let alone a proposal of marriage from the daunting Rafael Alvarados! Her mind had gone completely blank as soon as she had grasped his intention. 'I don't—I really——' was as far as she could get, then she made a tremendous effort to pull herself together and her voice was not on its normal steady course but slightly high-pitched as she tried again. 'You must see that I'm completely overwhelmed. I had no idea—I'm very grateful, of course—and honoured,' she added hastily as an afterthought, 'but marriage——!' This was said with such intensity that Rafael could not have missed the inward turmoil going through her thoughts at that time.

'It need not be so distasteful,' he said quietly yet thoughtfully, as if her reaction had given him food for thought, as well it might have done since Rafael had spent several years skilfully avoiding such a commitment. It was a new experience for him to find someone as wary of the marital state as he had once been. The fact that Mary was alone in the world and undeniably loved the boy she had looked upon as her own made her reluctance to accept his proposal even more startling.

He stared down at her; his past experience with the opposite sex and their intricate wiles to gain themselves a rich husband had not left a favourable impression on him, yet here was this woman now watching him with those large grey eyes of hers, plainly wanting to refuse his proposal. She was not beautiful, he mused, and could hardly be called pretty, yet she was not unpleasing to look at. He had called her attractive, and she was, he thought suddenly. Another thought then occurred to him that sent a wave of fury through him, surprising him with its depth of feeling. 'You told my father that you were free,' he said harshly. 'Was it a lie? Do you still care for the man you were engaged to?'

Mary stared up at him, no less surprised by his sudden change of mood. 'No,' she replied steadily. 'The engagement was ended. I told your father the truth.'

The reply appeared to please him and his voice lost its harshness as he said, 'This has come as a shock to you, of course, but I do ask you to seriously consider my proposal in the light of what I have told you. If you take everything into consideration, I believe that you will come to realise that it would be the perfect solution for the future. As I mentioned earlier, it need not be a distasteful experience. We can look upon it as a marriage of convenience, if you like. In time we may have second thoughts on the matter, so there will be no harm done. We shall just go our separate ways.'

If this calm statement was meant to assure Mary, it had the opposite effect, and a wave of panic rushed over her. He was taking it for granted that she would accept his proposal! In point of fact he was underlying her acceptance by laying down the rules of procedure after the marriage.

There were a lot of sacrifices she had had to make in the past where Enrique was concerned, but this was one that she felt utterly incapable of making. No doubt Isabel would think her quite mad in refusing to marry this dark handsome man whom she had pinned her hopes on for all these years, but then Isabel was not afraid of him, and Mary was. She knew he could be gentle and just with those he loved, this she knew instinctively, but he did not love her. In a way, she thought, he too, was making a sacrifice, but for whose sake? his father's or Enrique's? Had his father's slight relapse brought about a twinge of conscience? or had the fact that Isabel and Enrique simply did not get on force this decision on him?

It was probably a bit of each, she thought miserably, and then steeled herself to say what must be said. She must be firm or she would be lost. 'Señor Alvarados,' she began steadily, and was immediately stopped by Rafael who intervened with,

'I called you Mary. Please use my Christian name, too. I know you will find this difficult, but I really think we have got past the polite stage of our acquaintance.'

Mary was not quite sure what he meant by this, but there had been a certain inflection in his voice that started her heart palpitating at an alarming rate and almost made her forget her intention of firmly refusing his proposal, but not quite. However, her next attempt was forestalled by Rafael catching hold of her hand and placing it on his arm as he turned her back towards the villa again. 'Come, let us rescue Isabel from what she would consider an irksome duty. We shall say no more on the subject we have been discussing. There will be time enough for such arrangements.'

With a sinking heart Mary realised that she was no match for this very clever man. She was certain he had judged her reaction to a nicety, and had also known that she was on the point of refusing him when he had made that subtle intervention and had given her no time to voice her decision.

The only ray of hope that she was able to hold out to herself when she finally went to bed that evening was that she had not said 'yes' either, and if and when she ever got the opportunity of stating her case, then surely this would hold her in good stead? She hadn't actually lied to him, just agreed to think about it as he had suggested, so what was she worrying about? Only the fact that men like Rafael Alvarados usually got what they wanted, that was all, a tiny voice whispered in her brain.

CHAPTER TEN

THE following morning Don Emilio's doctor arrived and ordered a week's rest for him, and his confinement to bed gave Mary the excuse she badly needed to keep out of Rafael's way.

Unlike Isabel she did not consider sitting with Don Emilio and keeping him company an irksome task. She had grown very fond of him in the short time that she had resided in the villa, and judging by the smile of welcome she would always receive from him when she visited him in his room, his sentiments were the same as hers.

She would read to him from one of his favourite books, the English version, that was, for he had an admirable library selection in his study. On several occasions she would glance up at him to find that he had dropped off to sleep while she was reading to him, and then she would slip out of the room and return later to finish the chapter.

Whenever this happened he would always profusely apologise to her, and say with a twinkle in his eye that she had such a restful voice that she had lulled him to sleep but would she please wake him the next time, but of course Mary never did; sleep was essential for him if he was to regain his health.

This particular morning, however, he appeared to have something on his mind and whatever it was, it was worrying him.

When Mary asked him if he wanted her to read to

him and he refused with an impatient shake of the head she wondered if he would prefer to be alone, and she asked him if he wanted her to leave him.

This request brought a surprised look from Don Emilio as if that particular thought was furthermost from his mind, and then he gave her an apologetic smile. 'Sit down, Mary. I want to talk to you,' he said gently.

Mary now felt as worried as Don Emilio had looked, since she was certain that Rafael had told his father of his proposal to her and her obvious reluctance to accept it. There was no doubt in her mind that Don Emilio was about to add his sentiments on the matter and to urge her to accept.

'A little while ago,' he began slowly, fixing his dark eyes on Mary's now pale countenance, 'we talked of the future, and you were of the opinion that you felt that you would be unable to settle permanently here.'

Mary's large eyes left Don Emilio's and she looked at the counterpane on the bed. It wasn't going to be easy explaining why she had turned his son down—or rather why she would when the opportunity arose.

Don Emilio went on, 'I now want to ask you a question, and I want your honest answer, Mary. I am only seeking the truth. Has this decision of yours to eventually return to England anything at all to do with my son Rafael?'

Mary's eyes left the counterpane and flew to Don Emilio's. Whatever else she had expected him to ask her, it had not been this. Her flush must have given her thoughts away as she saw him give a slight nod of confirmation on his own thoughts on the matter.

'I thought so,' he said quietly. 'I must tell you now that I once harboured a wish that Rafael and you——'

he was silent for a moment or so, then said, 'But now I see that that was just wishful thinking.'

Mary's eyes searched his for a hint of duplicity, but she could see only tiredness in them. He did not know that Rafael had proposed to her, she thought. He couldn't know, and she was certainly not going to tell him. Her thoughts whirled about in her brain. She must tell him it wouldn't be fair not to, even though it meant that he was yet again to be disappointed since she had no intention of accepting him.

She swallowed quickly, 'Don Emilio,' she began quickly before her courage deserted her, 'I must——' was as far as she got as he gently patted her hand in a hushing gesture.

'Mary? You are fond of me, are you not?' he asked her suddenly, and at her swift nod, continued, 'I believe that you need Enrique, as much as he needs you,' he said quietly and Mary wondered if he was going to suggest that she break her promise to him and take Enrique back to England with her, and she knew quite suddenly that she was not going to allow Don Emilio to let her do any such thing. Enrique belonged here, and he was happy. She miserably wondered whether she ought to accept Rafael's proposal after all; it was better than hurting such a fine man as Don Emilio.

As if sensing her thoughts the old man gave her a weary smile. 'It is very selfish on my part, Mary, that makes me make what must seem to you to be an extraordinary request. I need Enrique, too, and I have come to rely on your soothing presence in my home.' He lifted up her small hand and held it lightly in his. 'I am asking you to stay, Mary, and I am asking you to accept my name.'

He gave a wry smile at her astounded countenance,

for surely, she thought, he was asking her to marry him! 'You see how desperate I am,' he added gently, 'to ensure your presence. As my wife you need have no fear of the future—or of Enrique's happiness. I am asking nothing more of you than your company, my dear, and the surety that you will stay.'

Mary's eyes filled with tears of gratitude for Don Emilio's kindness and she wished with all her heart she could accept this proposal, and maybe she would, she thought, but not until she had given Rafael his answer. How could she possibly tell Don Emilio about that now?

Her confusion was evident to Don Emilio, who patted her hand again as he said gently, 'Don't worry about it, Mary, but do think about it. Let the thought linger in your mind, and come and tell me when you have decided.'

'When you have decided', thought Mary later, in the blessed silence of her room. There were slight shades of Rafael's proposal in those few words. Not 'if you decide', in other words even Don Emilio in his gentle way had subtly bound her hands behind her back, making a refusal not only impossible, but impolite!

Somehow she had to tell Rafael of this new development since she would hate Don Emilio to suddenly find out that he had joined a queue of would-be suitors for her hand in marriage.

At this almost hysterical thought Mary walked across to the mirror on her dressing table and stared at her reflection. She saw no difference in her features; she was still plain Mary Allis with no pretensions to beauty. Rafael Alvarados had said her quietness was 'disturbing' and Don Emilio had said that she was 'soothing', but neither compliment, if they could so be called, seemed a good enough reason for marriage.

They were not, of course, she reminded herself sceptically, but Enrique was. She could not have done better, she told herself sadly, if she had been the mercenary woman Rafael had thought her, and perhaps would still think her when she told him of Don Emilio's proposal, and she must do that as soon as possible.

She did not envisage any trouble in that direction. If anything, Rafael would be highly relieved to have the pressure of Mary's future taken off his broad shoulders, and would probably congratulate them both with heartfelt relief. Would he then marry Isabel? she wondered, and she was surprised at the sudden stab of jealousy she felt at this thought. She hadn't wanted him to marry Isabel before, but she had thought it was because of Enrique—and it was, she assured herself fervently, not wanting to admit to herself that there could have been any other reason. But there was no denying that now that Enrique's happiness was assured, she still did not want him to marry Isabel!

She placed her hands under her chin and rested her elbows on the dressing table staring at her reflection as if seeking the answer there. Had she come to like him that much? she thought. Did she so dislike Isabel that she felt that she would not make him happy? Don Emilio had the same thoughts on the matter, she defended herself, so it was not just her. No, it couldn't have been jealousy that she had felt, she told herself; you only felt jealous when you loved someone—jealous of another woman, that was.

As it was Isabel's last night there, Mary chose her evening wear with more care than she had previously done. Only having the three evening dresses to choose from, she had nothing new to match the array of finery Isabel had brought with her. Mary had been in the hall when her cases had arrived and had wondered if she had come prepared to spend several months there instead of the few weeks mentioned.

Mary had not always worn evening dress, but had sometimes settled for one of her light summer three-quarter-length dresses, and this had helped to give her a little more variety. Tonight, she decided, she would wear the burgundy velvet dress. She had worn the other two dresses on different occasions, but she felt more comfortable in the velvet dress as she knew that it suited her.

If Mary had thought the previous evening's meal with Rafael and Isabel without the soothing presence of Don Emilio was uncomfortable, she soon discovered that there were different degrees of discomfort, and she wasn't sure which was worse, receiving Rafael's undivided attention, or Isabel's furious glares!

On the whole she would have preferred Isabel's glares, these she could contend with, but the look in Rafael's dark eyes as they rested on her was quite another thing. There was no doubt in Mary's mind that he was intent on willing her to accept his proposal. There was a strange magnetism in those looks of his that slightly frightened her. Almost, she mused, as if he looked upon her as his property already, and she knew with certainty that should Isabel throw a disparaging remark in her direction, she would receive the lash of a cutting remark from Rafael.

All, she mused bitterly, because of Enrique; her unhappy gaze rested on Isabel, dressed in a gorgeous gown of shimmering silver threads. Her lovely blue-black hair was drawn back from her oval face with its magnolia-tinted skin. Her large dark eyes were at that moment pleading with Rafael to stop pretending that he cared for the plain Englishwoman and look at her, for what attraction could such a woman hold for a man like him? If Mary's deductions on Isabel's thoughts were correct, then she heartily agreed with them, but she had forgotten the child.

When Rafael tried to coerce Mary into joining them on an evening stroll in the garden after dinner, Mary pleaded tiredness and a wish to go to bed. With Isabel there she knew she would have no opportunity of a private word with Rafael, and was disinclined to further infuriate Isabel by accepting.

Since Don Emilio was confined to bed, Mary called in on him before she retired, and found that she was not the only one with this intention in mind, for Rafael and Isabel were there too—Isabel for the sole purpose of thanking him for his hospitality, for she would be leaving early in the morning. It was plain that she had no wish to go, particularly as her stay had not brought about her cherished hopes of a proposal from Rafael.

When she saw Mary, Isabel's disappointment got the better of her good manners and she took her unhappiness out on Mary, who would be staying at the villa long after her departure. 'I don't suppose I shall be seeing you again,' she said with acid sweetness. 'You'll be gone before I make my next visit. I still don't envy you the English climate, but I'm sure you'd be happier there than here. It's what you're used to that counts, isn't it?'

It was not so much her choice of words as the implication behind them, and she had not been referring to the climate, Mary thought, but to the luxurious setting of the Alvarados home.

Mary saw no point in answering her since it was obvious that Isabel was a very unhappy woman and Mary felt a little sorry for her.

Don Emilio, however, had no such sentiments on the matter and highly resented Isabel's attitude to Mary. 'I believe you will find that your assumption that Mary would be happier in England totally incorrect. I sincerely hope so anyway, particularly as I have asked her to become my wife and have every hope of her acceptance,' he said stiffly, arresting Rafael's attention as he was hustling Isabel to the door to prevent any further unpleasantness.

Mary was only aware that for her time had stood still. There was a shocked hushed silence in the room that echoed not only her feelings but Rafael's and Isabel's, too. Isabel had her mouth open again, Mary noted abstractedly, her mind simply refusing to face up to the catastrophic result of Don Emilio's championship.

Her eyes flew to Rafael, and there was something in his tense stance that told her that far from being relieved of the necessity to provide for her future, he was absolutely furious. His searing gaze went from the quaking Mary to the proud determined face of his father, who could not have been unaware of the shock his statement had produced, and for a moment Mary sensed an antagonism between father and son that she had never dreamed was possible.

Rafael's gaze then returned to Mary, who wished she had the courage to run out of the room and bolt herself in her bedroom, such was the effect that his burning eyes had upon her, but her legs refused to move and she had to just stand there. 'And when,' he said softly but menacingly to her, 'did this proposal take place?'

As Mary was incapable of answering him, Don Emilio spoke for her. 'This morning,' he replied haughtily. 'Although I fail to see the reasoning behind your question.'

'You will,' promised Rafael harshly, 'when I tell you that I was under the impression that the lady had accepted my proposal, made,' he said, slowly emphasising the last word, 'last night.'

There was a strangled gasp from Isabel, who rushed out of the room with a speed that Mary envied and miserably wished that she could emulate. Her horrified eyes went from Rafael to Don Emilio. 'That's not entirely true,' she cried, and her eyes pleaded with Don Emilio to believe her. 'Rafael did propose to me, but I gave him no cause to assume that I had accepted him. I did promise to think about it, and that's an entirely different thing,' she said indignantly.

She saw Don Emilio's eyes rest on his son when she had finished, and watched a variety of emotions pass over his autocratic face. There had been amazement mingled with doubt, then a look of wicked amusement hastily masked when he met Mary's anxious eyes. 'I think you had better leave us, Mary,' he said gently. 'And do not worry, you will not be coerced into doing anything you do not want to do,' he promised.

On returning to her room, Mary found Isabel waiting for her. She was not at all surprised; after the events of the past hour she was beyond any expectation of peace.

'How clever of you,' purred the incensed Isabel. 'Tell me, which one will you choose? What does it feel like having two suitors to choose from?'

Mary surveyed Isabel's flashing eyes and highly flushed cheeks and the way her breast rose and fell in her emotional agitation. 'I think you know the answer to that better than I do,' she answered, deliberately avoiding the first question.

Isabel was not so easily put off. 'You haven't answered me!' she said, her voice rising on an hysterical note. 'Who is the lucky man, Rafael or Don Emilio?' she demanded.

Mary was coming to the end of her endurance. 'I fail to see what business it is of yours,' she replied coldly. 'I may not marry either of them.'

Isabel's harsh laugh rang out across the room, and Mary winced at its obvious implication. 'As if I would believe that!' she almost spat out at Mary. 'After all your hard work! The so quiet Mary Allis, tiptoeing about the place as if not to disturb anyone. Oh, yes,' she ground out at the swift look Mary gave her, 'I've noticed your little act of humble humility, and it worked, didn't it?' Her eyes were malicious as she added, 'If I were you I'd choose Don Emilio, it's my guess that Rafael only proposed to you because he'd some idea of what was in his father's mind.'

Mary watched her as she paced about the room in an attempt to contain her fury. 'And none of it would have happened if it hadn't been for that wretched child!' she burst out viciously. 'You do realise that, of course, don't you?' she hissed at Mary. 'For all your docile acts even Don Emilio would not have contemplated making such an unsuitable marriage, and Rafael would not have looked twice at you.'

'Might I remind you that "that wretched child", as you put it, happens to be Don Emilio's grandson, and Rafael's nephew,' Mary replied, now coldly furious herself at the way Isabel was blaming everybody but herself for her misfortune.

'Oh, I hadn't forgotten that part of it,' Isabel ground out. 'He wouldn't have married her, you know, no matter what you like to think, but it certainly gave you a rosy future, didn't it? Don Emilio wanted Rafael to marry me. Did you know that?' This was said in a whisper as her emotions thickened her voice, and as she met Mary's clear gaze she coloured and looked away quickly. 'He did!' she replied vehemently to Mary's unspoken challenge of this statement. 'I knew by the way he kept asking me questions when I sat with him last night.' She swallowed. 'I tried to tell him that Rafael wanted to marry me, but something was holding him back,' her voice caught in a sob. 'Now I know what it was, but Don Emilio knew, didn't he? That's why he asked you to marry him so that Rafael would be free to marry me.'

'Rafael is still free to marry you,' answered Mary wearily, 'if that's what he wants.' Her head was beginning to ache and she wanted to be left in peace.

A ray of hope gleamed in Isabel's eyes at this calm statement of Mary's. 'Does that mean that you will marry Don Emilio?' she asked almost eagerly.

Mary shook her head wearily. 'I've already told you that it's most unlikely that I'll marry either of them. You don't have to believe me and I'm sure that you don't, but there's nothing more I can add to that. Now will you please let me get some rest. It's been a long day.'

Isabel had to be content with this small crumb of comfort and grudgingly took her leave.

Mary's legs were weak as she sank down on her bed after Isabel had left. She now knew why Don Emilio had proposed to her. Isabel had been partially right, yet not wholly so. She recalled how worried he had seemed when she had visited him in the morning, and she now knew what had caused that worry—Isabel's wishful thinking! She could almost visualise the scene with Isabel pouring out her version of how it was with her and Rafael, and it must have been a convincing performance to make Don Emilio take the only action he could think of to preserve Mary's happiness.

Mary gave a sad smile. He hadn't believed her when she had said that she could walk off and leave Enrique when she felt the time was right. There would be no happiness for her without the child she had cared for all those years. He had also known that there was little chance of happiness for either her or Enrique, if Rafael married Isabel.

With his kindly insight he had taken full note of the fact that Enrique did not like Isabel, and vice versa, and there wasn't much one could do about that unless Isabel underwent a drastic change of character and put someone's happiness before her own.

As his wife, Mary would have a right to not only stay in Spain, but to watch over Enrique. A right that would give her precedence over any whim of Isabel's that might threaten his happiness, such as having him sent away to a boarding school at the earliest opportunity and out of her and Rafael's vicinity, and thus have Rafael to herself.

She gave herself a mental shake. These were hypothetical musings, but she was certain that Don Emilio's thoughts had been more or less on the same lines as hers. In which case, she thought ironically, she ought to seriously consider accepting his offer.

Her knees had not quite gained their flexibility when

she got up from the bed and started to prepare herself for bed. Her fingers were on the top of her dress zip when a loud rapping on the door made her still their action. She had no need to ask who was demanding entrance; only one person would invade her privacy at this time of night.

For a moment or so she thought that if she kept quiet he might assume that she had gone to bed and leave her in peace, but at his autocratic second round of raps she knew that if she did not let him in, he would rouse the whole house.

With hands that slightly trembled she opened the door to him, hoping that he would say what was on his mind outside the door, without the need to enter, but it was a forlorn hope as she watched him sweep into the room and calmly and deliberately close and lock the door behind him.

At this extremely worrying action of his Mary tried not to show her panic, assuring herself that all he was doing was making sure that they were not interrupted by Isabel who was just as likely to join them at any moment, considering that she must have heard Rafael's furious demand to speak to Mary, and where Rafael was concerned she had no inhibitions.

She glanced up at him briefly and then down at the floor, not liking the glint in his eyes as he stood in front of her with his feet planted slightly apart in a manner rather reminiscent of a tiger about to pounce on its prey.

'Are you going to marry my father?' he demanded without preamble, and Mary was surprised at the underlying fury in his voice.

She wished she could tell him to mind his own business, but the sad fact was that it was his business, and even if it wasn't, she wouldn't have the courage. She swallowed. 'Well?' he demanded angrily.

'I don't know,' she managed to get out, still refusing to look at him.

'I see,' he said furiously. 'You mean you are thinking about it, do you? Well, might I point out a few relevant facts that might not have occurred to you before. Do you realise that if you accept his proposal and not mine, you will become my stepmother?'

Mary blinked up at him as her tired brain assimilated this startling fact, then she closed her eyes, attempting to shut out an irresponsible but extremely amusing thought of what it would feel like to have him call her 'Mother'.

In her weak state she was totally unable to forestall the chuckle that escaped as her imagination took flight. The next moment he had grasped her shoulders in an iron hold and she winced as his steely fingers cut into her soft flesh.

'Think it's amusing, do you?' he ground out through clenched teeth. 'Then let's see how amusing you find this,' and he pulled her into his arms with a force that took her breath away.

The next minute he was kissing her in a way that no stepson should ever kiss his stepmother, but Mary was beyond any such thought. As soon as the initial shock had worn off, she found utter delight in the touch of his firm lips on hers. She didn't even mind the fact that the kisses were meant to punish her, as savage as they were she felt a surge of happiness flow through her and only wanted to cling with all her might to the man she now knew she loved with all her heart.

As suddenly as he had taken her in his arms he released her, leaving her feeling lost and bewildered as he stood looking at her through narrowed eyes, and there was a look of undisguised triumph in his that made her turn abruptly away from that all too knowing look of his and stare down at the floor.

She closed her eyes. He had made her feel a wanton. It wouldn't occur to him that she loved him, she thought bitterly. She was just another woman that he could manipulate by his sheer male dominance over her.

'Look at me, Mary,' he commanded autocratically.

Mary dumbly shook her head. He had got what he had wanted, she couldn't marry his father now. 'I can't,' she said in a low tone. 'Please go.'

He ignored her request and placed a long lean finger under her chin and made her look up at him. 'You can and you will,' he said softly. His eyes went searchingly over her face and then with the same deliberation that he had used before, he kissed her again. 'Now will you marry my father?' he queried softly.

Mary felt a wave of helplessness wash over her. He was willing to make love to her to save his father from falling into her clutches. 'Would you rather I went away?' she asked wearily, steadfastly meeting his eyes to show him that she had got the message and that there was no need for any further demonstration of affection from him.

'Yes, I would rather that than see you marry him—or anyone!' he added ferociously.

'Very well then,' she said dully, 'I shall make my arrangements.'

'You may safely leave all that to me,' replied Rafael magnanimously, and caught hold of her hand and lifted it to his lips. 'You will not regret it, Mary, I promise you.'

When he had left her Mary stood staring at the closed door. If the house had been on fire she still could not have moved from the position. She had known unhappiness before, but nothing like this. A short while ago two men had wanted to marry her, but each was intent on saving her from the other.

Don Emilio at least had had a selfless motive, but Mary had seen the look of relief that he had quickly masked when told of Rafael's prior claim to her hand.

She thought of Rafael's words that she would not regret her decision. He intended to make a substantial settlement for her co-operation obviously, and not only that, she thought wildly, he was even willing to arrange her swift departure from the scene! She could even imagine the scene at the airport with him thrusting a thick envelope into her hand just before she boarded her flight back to England.

'No!' she whispered vehemently; she wouldn't give him the satisfaction of seeing her off his territory—not even off his own premises!

With a calmness she had not thought herself capable of, she started packing, glad to have something to do to take her mind off the wretched situation that she now found herself in. She took everything but the three evening dresses that Rafael had so thoughtfully provided in order that she should not disgrace the family. Next she checked that she had her passport and money, and found with a sigh of relief that she had ample to cover her return journey, so there were no problems there.

Her next thought made her sit down abruptly on the bed again; how very clever of her, she thought bitterly. She had thought of everything but how she was going to leave the villa and get to the airport! She could not possibly ring for a taxi since the telephone was in the hall and the chances were that Rafael would come across her making the call, for it was his habit, she had noticed, to have a last cigar on the patio before retiring.

For the next few seconds she sat in a maze of despair; would nothing go right for her. Even when she tried to bow out of what had become an impossible situation, her escape route was blocked.

It was then that she thought of Joan Santos and a fresh wave of hope flowed over her. Joan would help her—she was certain of it!

Her mind made up, she went around the room making sure that she left it in good order, for she had an ingrained sense of tidiness. As she passed the larger of her two cases she thoughtfully picked it up and tested its weight. It was heavy, and by the time she had reached Joan's home she would know just how heavy it was. She sighed; well, she would just have to stop now and again and take a rest.

A glance at her watch told her that if she was going to arrive at Joan's before they retired for the night she would have to leave soon.

When she was finally satisfied that everything was in order and that she had everything that belonged to her, she opened the communicating door from her room to Enrique's and went quietly to the side of his bed and stood looking down at the sleeping child.

With no little concern she saw that he had been crying in his sleep, for the tear stains were visible on his flushed cheeks. As she watched him he gave a little yelp of fright; he was having a nightmare.

'Wake up, darling,' she said softly, and gently shook him awake. He opened two large sleepy eyes and blinked at her, then as the memory of the dream came back to him he clutched her fiercely. 'I'm not going to be a matador,' he said fervently.

Mistaking the reason for outburst and the bad dream he had had, she murmured comfortingly, 'They don't suffer long, darling, so it's not really as bad as it looks.'

Enrique plainly had not heard her, or if he had, her words had meant nothing to him. He shivered and buried his head in her breast. 'It was such a big bull,' he muttered, 'and so fierce, it nearly got him,' he shivered. 'I was frightened,' he said simply.

Mary gently pulled him away from her and gazed down into his puckered face. 'But he was all right, wasn't he?' she queried softly.

He nodded and gulped. 'Well then,' went on Mary, 'that's fine, isn't it? Matadors know what they're doing, pet. They wouldn't last long if they didn't. Do you want a hot drink?' she asked him quickly to take his mind off the subject.

He shook his head, and then grinned suddenly at her. 'Perhaps I will be a matador,' he declared stoutly, and the next minute he had snuggled down again and was soon fast asleep.

There were tears in Mary's eyes as she gazed down at him. He was his father's son all right. How proud Enrique would have been of him, not to mention Sheila.

At this thought her hands clenched by her side; she couldn't leave him. She looked down at the damp spot on her dress where his face had been pressed against it. He was not normally a demonstrative child. Wholly boyish, he hated any outward sign of affection, but on rare occasions would give her a fierce hug, telling her in a way that no words could convey that he loved her.

And here she was, Mary thought bitterly, on the point of walking out of his life simply because her pride had been hurt. Oh, there were other considerations, of course, but it all came down to that in the end, she thought, as she went back into her room and softly closed the door between them.

Her glance fell on her cases packed and ready to be picked up and taken with her on her flight from Spain, and she shook her head wearily at them. She would have to let Rafael do the arranging after all. There was Don Emilio, too, she thought sadly, and she wondered how she could have contemplated going without saying goodbye to him and thanking him for his kindness.

She passed a weary hand over her forehead; it seemed she hadn't been thinking straight, and no wonder, after the traumatic events of the evening.

Her shoulders squared. She would see Don Emilio in the morning and make it quite clear to him that she had no intention of marrying either of them, but was quite willing to stay at the villa in the capacity of companion to Don Emilio and mother to Enrique.

Not that this arrangement would suit Rafael, but Mary could see no other solution to the problem, and was too tired to come up with any other possibility.

She overslept the following morning, and found that Enrique had gone with Rafael and Isabel to Isabel's home. As she could not see Isabel inviting him along for the ride, Mary had an astute guess that Rafael had manoeuvred his presence to avoid any histrionics from Isabel, and to make certain that he returned to the villa at a reasonable hour.

Their absence was a relief for Mary, as she knew that she could now see Don Emilio and talk to him without fear of interruption from Rafael.

She ate a solitary breakfast on the patio, and re-hearsed what she would say to Don Emilio. She didn't want to hurt his feelings, but it was really time that she asserted her position, and she was forced to give a reluctant smile as she recalled Isabel's charge of her 'tiptoeing' about the place in the past.

To someone of Isabel's tempestuous nature, it must have appeared so to her, and Mary could quite understand why she had thought that it was all an act to ingratiate herself into the Alvarados's good books. She would not understand that it was Mary's nature to stay in the background.

It was after ten when Mary had finished her breakfast, and she was just debating whether to go for a walk and sit by the fountain until she could make her visit to Don Emilio, when the young maidservant appeared and told her that she was wanted on the telephone.

For a moment Mary wondered if the call was for Isabel and not her, for Isabel had received many calls during her visit. Her brows were raised in query as she asked the girl, 'For me?'

The girl nodded her head and smiled at Mary shyly. '*Si*, Señorita Allis,' she said firmly.

As Mary followed her back into the villa she wondered who could be ringing her, then she thought of Joan. Joan would know that Isabel was leaving that morning and had probably rung her to arrange a get-together. She had not seen Joan since Isabel's arrival and found herself looking forward to one of their homely chats; she had such a sensible outlook on life and at that moment in time Mary badly needed someone to talk to, and someone who would understand her dilemma.

She picked up the receiver expecting to hear Joan's voice on the other end of the line, and was surprised when a strange voice asked if she was speaking to Señorita Allis.

When Mary confirmed this, the woman then asked if it would be convenient for her if they came that afternoon to see to the fitting.

Mary stared at the receiver. She didn't know how it had happened, but it appeared that they had not only got the wrong number but the wrong Señorita Allis. 'I rather think you've got the wrong number,' she said, and waited for the usual apology, but it did not come; instead the woman asked, 'It is Señorita Mary Allis that I wish to speak to, are you not her?'

Mary blinked, and answered in a puzzled voice, 'Yes, I'm Mary Allis, but I know nothing about a fitting. A fitting for what?' she asked curiously.

The woman on the other end of the telephone gave a coy chuckle, 'These men,' she said, 'they are so anxious to get on with affairs! The Alvarados family have been patrons for this house for many years, and I can assure you that your wedding dress will be the finest that the house can offer.'

'Wedding dress?' queried Mary in a strangled voice. 'On whose orders?' she managed to get out, holding her breath for the answer.

'Señor Alvarados, of course,' replied the now affronted owner of the salon. 'Of course, if you want to place your order elsewhere——'

'Oh, no,' interrupted Mary hastily. 'I'm sorry, but could you tell me when this order was given to you?'

The woman was still puzzled, but she complied

readily enough. 'Why, this morning, *señorita*, and as we were given to understand that Señor Alvarados wishes the gown to be completed within a month, it is essential that we get an early fitting.'

The hall started swinging round in front of Mary's eyes and she had to clutch at the bureau that she was standing beside. How could Rafael have ordered a wedding dress for her that morning when he had agreed the previous evening that she should leave Seville?

Her spinning thoughts were halted by a plaintive, '*Señorita*, are you still there? Might I suggest three this afternoon for the first fitting?'

'I—very well,' replied Mary, trying to inject a note of authenticity into her voice. What did it matter when they came? Mary would just refer them to Rafael and he could tell them why their services would not be required, it was his worry, not hers!

Mary went up to her bedroom to give herself a little time to compose herself before she went to see Don Emilio. Questions were darting about in her head to which she had no answer. It simply did not make sense, not unless Rafael had had a brainstorm, and at this possible theory she slowly shook her head. If anyone was completely in control of himself it was Rafael Alvarados. She bit her lower lip; could Rafael have gone to see his father again after talking to her? Supposing he had, and Don Emilio had refused to let Mary go? Wouldn't that make him decide to go ahead and marry her himself?

Mary recalled how vehement he had been on the subject of her marrying Don Emilio, and positively savage on the question of her becoming his stepmother. She nodded her head slowly; yes, that alone was enough to force his hand since she would have precedence over any decision he made over Enrique in the future, and how he would hate that!

Now having sorted out things in her mind and certain that she had the answers, she tidied her hair and took a deep breath, then went down to see Don Emilio.

Don Emilio's welcoming smile made her give him an answering one, yet she had meant to be solemn and to show him that she had no intention of having her future arranged for her by the Alvarados's, no matter how kindly meant, where Don Emilio was concerned, anyway.

'And how is my future daughter-in-law feeling this morning?' he asked her with a twinkle in his eyes.

If anything was likely to give Mary a lead, that remark was. She eyed him sternly and answered with a gleam in her eye, 'I'm afraid I shall not become your daughter-in-law.' At his sudden look of consternation, she went on, more gently this time, 'Last night I told you that I was considering marrying Rafael, not that I had agreed. I also told you the truth when I said that I had given him no encouragement to believe that I would say yes to his proposal.' Her head was held high as she added firmly, 'Well, now I've decided. I shall not marry him,' she concluded on a note of finality. 'And as for your kind proposal,' her eyes lost some of their determination and she gave him an apologetic smile, 'I'm honoured that you should have asked me, but honestly there was no need, you know. I shall be perfectly happy staying and keeping you company.' She gave a light shrug of her slim shoulders. 'I was wrong in thinking I could walk off and leave Enrique. You knew that, didn't you? and that was why you thought you ought to propose to me, to keep me here.' She patted his hand lying on the counterpane. 'Well, you have no need to worry about it. I shall stay, I promise.'

Don Emilio gave her a thoughful look, and to her extreme embarrassment asked her the one question she would least want to answer. 'Mary, do you love my son?'

Mary's cheeks flamed and she looked away quickly from his searching eyes, afraid that he might read the truth in hers.

'I have a particular reason for asking this,' he went on steadily, 'because if the answer is no, then I would advise you to go back to England.'

Mary's startled eyes flew to his, and he gave her another searching look. 'He loves you, Mary,' he said, and his voice sounded tired as he added gently, 'and as much as I want you to stay, I know that he will give you no peace until you agree to marry him.' He smiled sadly. 'He will browbeat you into acceptance—he is not a man to be denied once he has set his mind on a goal.'

Mary tried to speak, but words were beyond her; she simply could not believe what Don Emilio was telling her. She desperately wanted to, but she couldn't.

'You find it hard to believe, don't you?' said Don Emilio slowly. 'I'm too fond of you, Mary, to try to deceive you. You ought to know that of me at least,' he added gently. 'I only want what's best for you. I can imagine how Rafael's attentions must have affected you—he would be no gentle or patient lover.' He gave her another small smile. 'And my poor Mary would bolt for the nearest hole. I'm right, aren't I?' he asked.

Mary swallowed and lifted up her head in an action that said more than words. 'If he loves me,' she said simply, 'then I shall not look for a bolthole.'

Don Emilio's hand caught hers and he held it tight

in his. 'I thought I hadn't been mistaken in you,' he said softly. 'If I were younger then I might not have stood down for my son. He is a good man, Mary, and I have no hesitation in advising you to accept him as a husband.'

Mary's grey eyes met the old man's earnest ones, but there was a shadow in hers. 'If he loves me,' she said quietly, 'why did he agree with me when I suggested that I should go away?'

For a moment Don Emilio was taken aback, then he said, 'When did you make this suggestion? And what preceded it? Tell me the whole of it,' he urged.

Mary told him of Rafael's visit to her the previous evening, and how he was intent only on making her agree not to marry his father. She stumbled a little in the telling, but she knew that Don Emilio would guess at the method chosen by Rafael to achieve his aims. 'I then asked him,' went on Mary, 'if he would rather I went away, and he said yes, he would rather that than see me marry you—or anyone.' When she came to this part she stopped suddenly and gazed wide-eyed at Don Emilio as if something had just occurred to her. 'Or anyone,' he had said. Anyone but him, he had meant, and she had thought——

'He was warning you, Mary, that if you refused to marry him it would be better for you both if you left, but I told you that, didn't I?' said Don Emilio. 'Not that I can imagine him letting you do any such thing,' he added dryly, 'not if I know my son.' He gave her a wicked smile. 'You might as well give in, you know,' he warned her gently.

'He said I was not to worry about the arrangements,' she murmured in a wondering voice, still marvelling at the way she had completely misunderstood his words.

She had been thinking of travel arrangements and he of wedding arrangements!

Her heart soared as she left Don Emilio later that morning, and too excited to want to bother about lunch she made her way to her favourite spot beside the fountain.

As she gazed dreamily at the sparkling drops of water as they cascaded down, she felt that she was in another world, a world where fairy stories came true, where anything and everything could happen.

Lost in her dreams, she did not hear the firm step of the man she was dreaming of, and gave a little cry of surprise when she found herself lifted from the seat and held in two strong arms. Her large grey eyes were still full of daydreams as they met the dark searching ones of Rafael.

'Tell me, *amada*, of what do you dream?' he asked huskily.

His *amada* laid a light finger on her lips and then placed it caressingly on his. The action told him everything that he wanted to know, and with a swift inward breath he bent his lips to hers. 'I can do better than that,' he said, and did!

FREE
Harlequin
romance
catalogue

A complete
listing of all the
titles currently available through
Harlequin Reader Service

Harlequin's Collection . . .

Harlequin Presents...

Harlequin Romances

Harlequin Reader Service

IN U.S.A.:   MPO Box 707, Niagara Falls, N.Y. 14302
IN CANADA: 649 Ontario St., Stratford, Ontario N5A 6W2

Don't miss any of these exciting titles.

Complete and mail this coupon today!